**Coming soon from Chantal Fernando
and Carina Press**

Knights of Fury MC

Renegade
Temper

Also available from Chantal Fernando

Wind Dragons MC

Dragon's Lair
Arrow's Hell
Tracker's End
Dirty Ride
Rake's Redemption
Wild Ride
Wolf's Mate
Last Ride
Crossroads

Cursed Ravens MC

Ace of Hearts
Knuckle Down
Going Rogue

Conflict of Interest

Breaching the Contract
Seducing the Defendant
Approaching the Bench
Leading the Witness

For Natty.

I miss you.

Every day.

SAINT

_____

CHANTAL FERNANDO

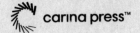
carina press™

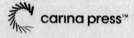

carina press™

Recycling programs
for this product may
not exist in your area.

ISBN-13: 978-1-335-21581-9

Saint

Copyright © 2019 by Chantal Fernando

All rights reserved. Except for use in any review, the reproduction or
utilization of this work in whole or in part in any form by any electronic,
mechanical or other means, now known or hereafter invented, including
xerography, photocopying and recording, or in any information storage
or retrieval system, is forbidden without the written permission of the
publisher, Harlequin Enterprises Limited, 22 Adelaide St. West, 40th Floor,
Toronto, Ontario M5H 4E3, Canada.

This is a work of fiction. Names, characters, places and incidents are
either the product of the author's imagination or are used fictitiously,
and any resemblance to actual persons, living or dead, business
establishments, events or locales is entirely coincidental.

This edition published by arrangement with Harlequin Books S.A.

® and TM are trademarks of the publisher. Trademarks indicated with
® are registered in the United States Patent and Trademark Office, the
Canadian Intellectual Property Office and in other countries.

www.CarinaPress.com

Printed in U.S.A.

SAINT

Chapter One

Age 10

"What's wrong, Sky?" my dad asks as I step into the clubhouse with a sad face, my pink backpack dragging behind me. My body language screams defeat, and even I know it. "Bad day at school?"

I nod at my father. Technically, he's my stepfather, but considering I never knew my biological father, Hammer's the only father I've ever known. He started dating my mom when I was just a baby. My mother has never told me about who my real dad is, and I've always wanted to know. Especially since she's so secretive about it. I don't care too much, though. I have Hammer.

"I guess you could say that."

I've been finding it hard to make friends. No one wants to play with me because they know my stepdad is in a motorcycle gang. I'm not sure why they all hate bikers. I know and love every person in this clubhouse, and they are always nice to me. I don't live in the clubhouse, but we come here pretty much every day after school. Hammer plays basketball with me and my siblings, and is always there for me no matter what. Does it matter that he chooses to ride a motorcycle instead of driving a car, or a van, like most of the other parents? Not to me, but apparently it does to them.

"Tell me what happened," he murmurs in a calm tone, but I know Dad gets mad at anyone who upsets me. I'm the youngest of six, and everyone loves to baby me. I'm also the only girl. Yeah, I feel sorry for myself too.

I sit next to him on the weathered brown leather couch. Before I can say anything, my mother speaks for me. "She got into a fight and is now suspended from school." She looks at me in frustration. "I told you that you need to stay out of trouble, Sky."

I grit my teeth in anger. Anger that she doesn't understand what it is like for me. Anger that she's talking for me. Mom lectured me on the whole drive back here, and now she's going to get Dad on her side before I can even get a word in. "But—"

"Fighting isn't the answer," she continues, shaking her head in disappointment. "I know you've been raised with boys, but you're a lady, and ladies don't fight."

"Didn't you slap that woman at the cookout last month, Georgia?" Dad asks with a smirk, brown eyes alive with mischief. He runs his fingers down his dark beard and nods. "Pretty sure you did. In front of the whole club."

"I saw that," I add, lifting my chin.

My mother scowls, sending a death stare in my direction. "What have I told you? Do as I say, not as I do."

"Becky deserved it, Mom," I say, trying to explain, and wanting my dad to understand. "She said her daddy is dead and it's our fault. He was a policeman. How would that be our fault? So I called her a liar and hit her. She shouldn't be talking bad about my family."

Dad and Mom share a look, one I can't figure out.

My mom has always told me "Do as I say, not as I do," but I can't help it if I'm the way that I am. I want to protect myself and my family.

Dad gives me a big hug. I close my eyes and sink into him, knowing that I'm safe in his arms. "You're not in trouble, Sky," he assures me gently. "But you shouldn't get into any more fights, okay? You're at school to get an education, not to get into trouble."

"I know," I grumble. "I'll try not get into any more fights."

"Promise?" he asks, pulling away and offering me his pinky finger. "We know you are going to do great things with your life. Things far away from here. But to do that, you need to be good in school, and to keep your grades up."

I wrap my pinky around his and squeeze. "I promise. I'll be good."

Funny that I'd make that promise to him, but not to my mother.

Chapter Two

Age 15

"What are you doing here?" Saint asks as I step inside the clubhouse, frowning as he takes in my denim shorts and white top. "And dressed like that?"

I roll my eyes at him. I've known Saint for about three years now, and normally I'd think of him as a friend, just another one of the guys. Okay, that's a lie. I've always thought he was good looking—in fact, he's probably the hottest guy I know in real life—but it was always just in a "yeah, he's cute" type of way. But recently something has changed. My heart beats faster when he's around, and I want to look nice for him. I even put on a little makeup before I got here.

It's time I admit that I have a crush on Saint, a crush that is completely one-sided.

Before we could hang out and everything would be normal, but now I get nervous every time he's around, and I think it's because I'm now seeing him in a different light. I wish things would just go back to the way they were before, because we'd just chat, give each other shit or watch movies or something, but now I'm awkward around him and don't know how to act.

Let's add that he's five years older than me and a prospect for the Knights of Fury MC.

The MC my father is president of.

So basically, he's never going to see me as anything more than Hammer's daughter. I need to nip this little crush in the bud as soon as possible, because it's a huge inconvenience to my life.

"What do you mean, what am I doing here?" I ask him, brow furrowing. I walk into the kitchen, and he follows behind me, eating a green apple. "Isn't the party tonight?"

"The party got canceled. Georgia didn't tell you?" he asks as he takes another bite, white teeth flashing, then hops up on the countertop with me standing in front of him.

"No, she didn't," I reply, shrugging. "Oh well, where's Dad then?"

"He's got some business going on here today, which is why I'm surprised that you're here," he continues, pausing and studying me. "Your eyes look really green today."

I narrow said eyes. "Are you okay?"

He jumps down and leans over to put his apple core in the garbage, his body close to mine, but not touching. He's so much taller than my five foot five, and I have to look up to see his face. Blue eyes watch me. He's always watching. There's something about him, about the way he looks at me, like he can see into my soul. It's intense, and almost a little too intense. I wonder if he looks at everyone this way, if maybe it's just who he is. I look away, like I always do, and take a step back.

"I'm fine. How about you? How did your exams go?" he asks, now leaning back against the counter with his arms crossed against his broad chest. With his shoulder-length dark hair, olive skin and those piercing baby blues, it's no wonder he has so many girls after him. I've seen it with my own eyes, once when he took me to the mall, and any time we have a family-friendly party at the club-house that I'm allowed to attend. Like a moth to a flame, if Saint is around, he has women around him.

I hate it.

If jealously is that burn in your chest and that feeling of dread in your stomach, then yeah, I've got that. I don't say anything, though. I mean, I can't. Nothing has happened between us, and I'm a child compared to him. He probably doesn't even look at me like that; I'm sure my dad would kill him even if he did. I really hope he doesn't see me as a younger sister, though, because I already have more than enough older brothers than I can handle.

"I aced them," I reply with a wide, smug smile.

"Well done," he compliments, a grin playing on his full lips. "I'm sure it has nothing to do with the new phone Hammer promised you if you passed them all."

"Nothing at all," I reply with a straight face. "You know, it won't be long until I'm finished with school," I remind him, shifting on my feet. Before I know it, I'll be eighteen too. I wonder if that will make any difference to him. I sure as hell hope so. Maybe he will start seeing me in a different light. A girl can dream.

"I know," he replies, looking up at the ceiling. "What are you going to do then?"

While he's looking away, I take him in from head to toe. Dressed in all black, as usual, a V-neck T-shirt, jeans and boots. He has a leather cuff around his wrist, one I know doubles as a manly scrunchie.

"What was the question again?" I ask, licking my suddenly dry lips.

"Don't look at me like that, Skylar," he says with an expression on his face that I can't seem to decipher.

"Like what?" I ask, glancing down and taking a deep breath.

Before he can answer, my dad walks into the kitchen, empty beer in hand. "What you doing here, Sky?"

I purse my lips and turn to him. "What a warm welcome everyone is giving me today."

Dad grins and wraps a big arm around me. He's such a huge man, when I was little he used to remind me of the Hulk. "You know I love having you here. It's just that today we have the other chapter coming in."

"Is that why the party was canceled?" I ask, glancing between Saint and him.

Ever since I became a teen, my dad doesn't like me being here whenever anyone else outside of this chapter is around, so I usually just stay home. I live with my mom and one of my brothers, Brooks, who is closest in age to me, but still four years older. The two of us are like water and oil—we don't mix, and we never have. I have four other older brothers: Logan, Seth, Axel, and Smith. All of them, including Brooks, have the same father, some guy none of them talk to anymore. I have a different biological father; but no one knows who he is. Every time I've asked Mom about him, she has deflected and not given me a proper answer.

"Yeah, I told Georgia to tell you," he continues, making a *tsk tsk* noise with his tongue. "How did you get here?"

"Brooks dropped me off on his way to basketball."

Dad turns to Saint. "Can you give her a ride home?"

He nods. "No problem."

Dad kisses the top of my head. "I'll see you tomorrow, Sky."

"All right, Dad," I say, bummed about the fact there will be nothing going on tonight for me, no amazing food or company, I'll probably end up being home alone watching TV and binge eating pizza. I suppose I could call up one of my friends to come over and hang out with me, but it won't be as interesting.

Saint and I walk outside, heading toward his bike. I try not to get too excited, but he glances back at me, taking in my attire. "Yeah, let's take the car."

Damn it. I was looking forward to getting on his motorcycle, and it would have been for the first time. I've only ever ridden with my Dad or Temper, one of the other members of the MC, and no one else.

"Fine," I say with resignation, knowing I would have frozen my butt off if we had taken the bike.

He opens the car door for me, which surprises me, and waits until I slide in before he moves to the driver's side. I look up and into the mirror, fixing my long red hair and pushing it back behind my ear as he gets in.

"You look fine" he murmurs, not looking at me.

I close the mirror and eye his profile. "Thank you."

Tension fills the car, and I shift on my seat, swallowing hard. Saint starts the engine and turns on the radio. "Still listen to sheep music?" he asks me, amusement in his tone.

I roll my eyes. "Just because I like listening to the top fifty doesn't make me a sheep. It means I have good taste, because I happen to like popular music. What does that make you then? Liking non-mainstream music doesn't make you any better."

"It makes me a wolf," he replies, flashing his perfect white teeth.

At that very moment, "She Wolf" by Shakira fills the car, and I start to laugh, unable to stop myself.

He shakes his head at me and pulls out of the clubhouse parking lot.

He's more than just a wolf.

He's a Knight.

And that means so much more to me.

Chapter Three

Age 16

"Who is that with Saint?" I ask Brooks, scowling as I see the woman rest her palm on his chest.

"Why? She's hot, isn't she?" he says, smacking his lips together. "Saint always picks up the hottest chicks."

That is literally the last thing I want to hear. And I'm sure my brother knows it. He's such an asshole sometimes.

"She's just a hanger-on," I mutter under my breath, glancing over the yard, and then looking up at the sunset to distract myself. I don't need Saint to catch me sending daggers in his direction. It's my eldest brother's birthday party, and I need to focus on that and only that. "Where's Logan?"

"He's on his way," Brooks says, shrugging. "You know Logan. He only comes to these things because Mom makes him."

Not all of us embraced the MC lifestyle. Logan left the second he turned eighteen, and now we pretty much only see him on birthdays and holidays. I know he loves us—he just never fit in here at the clubhouse, and prefers a quieter, private lifestyle. And as he calls it, a less criminal one.

Our family is big, and complicated, but we try our best to make things work and include everyone, even if the birthday boy himself hasn't even shown up yet, and my crush is standing a little too close to some pretty brunette for my liking. I hate that it has to be that way, and there's nothing I can do about it. I'm younger than him, and he sees me as some kid. Yet when we hang out, there's just something there that makes me want to be around him. He shows a different side of himself to me, a side that the rest of the world doesn't see. Maybe it's one-sided, but I have to hope when I'm older, things will be different for us. If not for the brunette.

I decide to head back inside—ignorance is bliss and all of that—and help my mom with the food. "Who made these?" I ask, picking up one of the little mini quiches. "They look delicious."

"I did." She beams, standing up from the oven and turning to me. "I made everything except the cake. Can you call Logan and see where he is? I was thinking we could sing happy birthday to him the second he walks through the door."

It's kind of weird being at a birthday party without the birthday boy, so I agree to call him and see where he is, not that the men here need a reason to party. It will be nice to see Logan, even though he doesn't love being at the clubhouse. He always looked after me growing up, and I do love and miss him. I think because he was the firstborn child, my mom does seem to make more of an effort with him and hates that he has this new life without us. She tries everything to get him to come around more.

"How old is he today again?" I ask, wrinkling my nose and pulling out my new phone from my jean pocket.

"Twenty-nine," she replies, eyes widening. "Wow, I almost have a thirty-year-old."

I hit Logan's name and listen to it ring and go to voicemail. "He's not answering."

"Must be driving," she replies absently.

"Anything else you need me to do?" I ask her, looking around the kitchen.

I have a weird relationship with my mom. We get along, but at the same time we're not very close. We don't seem to understand each other or have any type of the connection I've seen some of my friends have with their mothers. I've always gotten the impression that she wished she had all boys, maybe because she seems to favor all of them. Either way, I'm definitely not her favorite child. In fact, I'm most likely her least.

Hammer makes up for it, though. He is always there for me when I need him, making sure I'm okay and spending time with me. He teaches me new things, laughs at my jokes and is slow to anger. I appreciate him more than he knows.

"No, I've got it under control, Sky. You can keep trying to get in touch with Logan, though," she says, her focus already shifting to whatever dish she's fussing over now.

"Okay," I reply, heading for the living room, and dropping down onto the couch, trying my brother again. When he still doesn't pick up, I expel a deep sigh and rest my head back on the velvet pillow.

"Come here to hide out too?" asks Temper, my dad's friend and the Vice President of the Knights.

"Oh my god," I groan, hand on my heart. "You scared the shit out of me, Temper. Jesus Christ."

He simply grins, arching his brow at me in an amused manner from where he's perched on the opposite couch. "You allowed to cuss now?"

I stick my tongue out at him. "I'm almost grown now, man. I can do what I want, when I want."

We both share a laugh, because we know just how untrue that happens to be.

"You're funny," he says, brown eyes smiling. "You know that? I don't know where you got your personality, because it definitely wasn't from your mother."

I laugh out loud. "Yeah, she's not the funniest woman I've ever met."

In fact, I don't think she's ever told a joke or made me laugh uncontrollably. That's more my dad's job, or even Saint's. Saint can be pretty funny when he wants to be, and has a quiet yet dry type of humor, which I can appreciate.

"I'm funny *and* cute," I add, batting my lashes slowly. "How lucky I am."

Temper throws a pillow at me. "Try that shit in a few years, and I'm sure you'll have all the men on their knees." He pauses, and then adds, "Actually, none of the Knights, but you know, other men."

His comment strikes a chord with me. I've never wanted just anyone. The only man I have my eyes on happens to be in this clubhouse right now. They always say stuff like this to me, about how I'm going to get them all into shit, because I'm pretty and have a mouth on me, and how I'm trouble waiting to happen. I don't think that's the truth, though.

I lift my chin in indignation. "Are you guys really going to let me date a man who isn't a Knight?"

Because I can't see that happening. The boys at school are nothing but my friends, and it's gotten to a point where no one even bothers to ask me out because they all know I'm going to gently refuse them. I don't think I'm better than them in any way, I'm just not interested. I can't help my pull toward Saint. It's torture, and it probably won't end well, but I can't help how I feel about him. Temper doesn't speak for the whole MC, and even if he would prefer I not date any of the Knights, that doesn't mean it can't happen.

"Why the hell would you want to do that?" the man I was just thinking about asks as he walks in and sits next to me, the scent of his cologne hitting my nostrils and sending me into overdrive. "All the good men are right here."

"I don't know about good." Temper winces, tilting his head to the side, brown eyes studying me. "Badass, maybe. Good? Probably not."

None of the men inside these walls consider themselves good men. However, I've seen good in all of them, and continue to do so. They are kind to me, patient, and treat me as if I'm a family member. If that's not the definition of good, then I don't know what is, but I love them all just the way they are.

"Everyone is good to me," I reply on a shrug.

"Only because Hammer would kill us if we weren't." Temper smirks, throwing another pillow at me.

"Can you not?" I ask him, scowling. "I know they call you Temper, but you're about to see mine."

I've noticed something about Temper. The men are wary of him, and always make sure never to push him too far. I've never seen him lose his shit, but I've heard the stories, and with his large build I can see why they wouldn't want to mess with him. To me, I see him as more of the strong and silent type. He acts silly with me, and is protective, but I think that's because he sees me as a niece or something. He keeps an eye on me, but likes giving me shit too. I like him. We have good chats and he's someone I trust.

Saint chuckles from next to me, and the sound brings my attention straight back to him. "Hammer raised a little hellion."

Saint says it like it's a good thing, and when he looks over at me, I get lost in his blue eyes. They are my weakness, not that I'd ever admit that out loud.

"Would you expect any different?" Temper replies in a dry tone, then glances at Saint, a contemplative look on his face. "Thought you were with Diana. What's happening there?"

Why does Temper have to do that? I know that everyone is a little weird about Saint and me hanging out, or even us being alone together, but nothing ever happens. We just chat and joke around. He doesn't even flirt with me, not that I don't try. I guess he saves that other side of himself for women like Diana.

Saint's blue eyes are suddenly looking everywhere except at me. "We were just chatting, that's all."

"Hmmmm," Temper replies, narrowing his gaze. He is always suspicious. Maybe he thinks something is going on with us, and I wish that were true. Unfortunately, Saint hasn't so much as held my hand even when we've been alone and had the opportunity.

"Why are you being all cryptic?" I ask, looking between the two men who are having a silent conversation. I am completely lost now. "Does Diana have an STD or something?"

Low blow, I know, but I have to get my kicks somehow.

Temper barks out a laugh, his wide shoulders shaking. "Fucking hell, Sky. You're so young, you know that?" He pauses and then adds, "But maybe he *should* be worried about that."

"Seriously?" Saint mutters, jaw suddenly tense. "Thanks, Temper."

"Compared to you I'm young, I guess," I reply to Temper, ignoring Saint.

Temper laughs harder.

"Ignore him," Saint says to me, his voice instantly drawing me in, Temper and his shenanigans forgotten.

I asked him once why they call him Saint when I know for a fact his name is Thorn Benson. He said it's because compared to all the other men here, he *is* a Saint.

I call bullshit.

I might be young, and maybe even naïve, but I'm not stupid.

"I always do," I reply, snuggling back into the couch. "Logan isn't even here, and he's not picking up the phone. We might just be having this party in his honor, without his presence. I don't know why Mom bothered— she knows he doesn't even like coming here."

Another day, another dysfunctional family issue.

I think Mom was hoping, even pressuring, Logan to join the Knights of Fury MC, but in the end it backfired, and now he wants nothing to do with them. She needs to let go, as he's already chosen his own path. My mother, though, is known for her tenacity.

"Ahh well, I'm just here for the food anyway," Temper

replies, standing up, his height making him look like a giant. "Speaking of."

We watch him walk away, leaving the two of us momentarily alone.

Probably not the best idea, at least not for me, because suddenly I'm finding it hard to think of something to say. I hate how it's become so hard for us to talk. It never used to be like this before.

Lucky for me, Saint speaks first. "It's not on you if your brother doesn't show up. You know he's not a fan of being here. I don't know why your mom bothers with the big parties, pretending we're all one big family."

"I know," I reply, glancing down. "We should have just done something else with him. It's like she makes it about her instead of him and what he wants."

"I think we all know the party is more for your mom than Logan, like you said. But Temper is right, at least there's good food. There's always a silver lining, and if that lining is lining my stomach I'm not going to complain."

Saint says this as he wraps his arm around me and kisses my temple. He can be affectionate, sometimes, but never in the way I crave. More like a big brother. Unfortunately. But I still enjoy times like these, knowing it's more than he gives anyone else. "You're the rose that came from concrete, do you know that?"

I'm about to ask him exactly what he means by that when my dad walks in, barking out Saint's name. I assume he's about to yell at him for being so close to me, something we do avoid when he is around, but I know I'm wrong when he says something that sends a shiver up my spine.

"Get all the men together. We have a fuckin' problem, and we need to handle it right now."

And then Saint's up, doing what he's told, and I'm left alone wondering what the hell is going on. I know they will never tell me, though. They let me in on the good times but shield me from the bad, even though I know there is plenty of bad. Sometimes I'm curious about what's going on, and other times I just block it out and leave them to it. This is their lives, and what do I know about how an MC works? As interested as I am, I don't really want to know. At least not now.

I'm just here for the family and food.

I try Logan again and he finally picks up, and before I can say hello, he yells into the line, "I'm not fuckin' coming, Sky. Tell Mom again, since she didn't listen the first ten times. Thank you, and I love you."

He hangs up, and I stare at my phone for a few moments. Well, at least he said he loved me. I don't know why Mom does this every time—she can't push Logan to be a part of something he doesn't want to. She chose the MC life, not him, and he's old enough to do whatever the hell he wants now.

The drama.

Sometimes I can see why our biological fathers left us all.

I sleep at the clubhouse that night, which isn't unusual, especially for weekends, but loud voices wake me up and I can tell that something is very wrong.

When I overhear my name, I go out to the kitchen to see what all the commotion is about. My mom is at the kitchen table with Hammer opposite her, but won't even look at me, too lost in thought.

"What's wrong?" I ask.

All conversation stops between Hammer and Mom the second they realize that I'm there, which lets me know it's something they don't want me to overhear. Damn, I should have stayed hidden and just listened in.

"Go to bed, Sky," my mom demands, tone laced with impatience and irritation. She looks away, like she expects me to just follow her orders instantly, and like I'm simply going to do as I'm told. Something in my gut tells me that something isn't right, though, and I need to know what's going on, especially if it involves me. Has something bad happened? Is someone hurt? My brothers? Saint?

"I heard my name," I explain, glancing between the two. "Is everything okay?"

My dad won't look at me, his eyes darting down to his hands in front of him. I don't know why he's remaining silent right now, when it's so unlike him. Hammer does and says whatever he likes; it's one of the things I love about him.

Why won't he look at me?

"It's fine," she replies curtly, glancing over before turning her back on me once more. "This is adult business, and you need to go back to bed."

Adult business that apparently involves me.

Hammer, who usually stands up for me any time my mom gets into one of her evil moods, continues to say nothing, but his tight jaw lets me know he's unhappy about something.

Feeling hurt, I leave the kitchen and walk back down the hallway, except this time I stop in front of Saint's door. I lift my hand to knock, but can't find myself quite able to. It's not like this is something I've ever done before, and I don't know if he would appreciate it or not. If he also tells me I should just go to bed, I think I might scream. I move to turn and just head back to my room, but then the door opens.

"Sky? What are you doing still awake?" he asks me, standing there shirtless, in nothing but some shorts. His body is amazing, muscles so defined, so deadly, he has turned himself into a weapon.

A beautiful one.

"Can't sleep," I tell him, glancing behind him with curiosity. "I'm not interrupting anything, am I?"

His eyes narrow slightly. "No, I'm just watching TV. Do you want to come in?"

I look around the hallway to make sure no one is around, then nod and enter his domain. I've never been in his room before. He has a massive wall-mounted TV and his bed looks comfortable as hell, all black bedding and plush pillows.

"Not what I was expecting," I admit as I sit on the very edge of the bed and look at the TV. "What are you watching?"

"*Supernatural*," he says, leaving the door open a bit and passing me the remote. He then opens a drawer and pulls out a black T-shirt, sliding it over his head and covering the amazing view. "But we can watch whatever you want."

He doesn't ask me what the hell I'm doing here, which is nice, because I don't know if I have an answer for that. It's almost as if I'm crossing a line here, or changing the rules on our friendship.

"Really?" I ask, arching my brow. "Just like that, huh?"

"Guest picks," he replies with a smirk. "I'm giving you the remote, not my credit card; calm down, Sky."

I have a laugh at that. "For now," I add cheekily.

He shakes his head and picks me up, moving me farther onto the bed. "You don't have to sit with one butt cheek off the bed—get yourself comfortable."

I do as he suggests, but don't lie down. Instead I sit perched on a few of his pillows and look for something for us to watch. When I settle on a romantic comedy, I expect a complaint from him, but he stays quiet and lies down next to me.

"What happened tonight?" I ask him quietly as the movie starts to play.

"Club business, Sky," is all he gives me. "Don't worry, we will take care of it, like we always do."

"Mom and Dad were fighting, and I heard my name," I admit to him, hoping that he can offer me some insight, or some answers. Anything.

"I'm not sure what that was about, but you know them two, they're always arguing about something or another," he says, lifting the blanket up over me. "Don't stress about it."

I try not to, and soon get lost in the movie.

It's not long before I fall asleep, cuddled up next to him, not a worry in the world.

I wake up to an empty bed and screaming.

I jump out of Saint's bed, the last place I want to be found—not like anything happened, but it's still not good. I rush toward the noise. My dad, Saint and my mom are yelling at each other.

"You can't do this!" Saint yells, starting to pace. "Hammer, you can't let her do this!"

"She's my daughter," my mom growls in a smug tone.

When she sees me, she barks out, "Get your shit, Sky, we're leaving."

I lock eyes with Saint, who looks panicked, and almost scared.

"Don't do this," Dad pleads with her. "Leave Sky here. I'll look after her. And you know I'll take good care of her."

Confusion fills me. Leave me here? Where is Mom going? I don't know what's happening, but my first instinct is to scream yes, let me stay with Dad. I want that. I want to stay with Hammer. My father. The only father I've ever known.

"I'm not leaving my daughter behind," Mom sneers, lifting her chin. "She's just your stepdaughter, Hammer, she's not your blood, so don't even think of trying to take her, or the police will be here before you know it. And you know what I'll tell them, so don't push me. You're a dead man walking, anyway. What's the point? I tried to help you, and you didn't want it. Now you can deal with the consequences."

"That was your idea of helping me?" he growls, anger filling his gaze. "You disgust me, Georgia. And Skylar deserves so much fucking better. If you love her at all, you will leave her here! For one second stop thinking about yourself and do what is best for her."

"Go get your bag, Sky!" she yells once more. I rush to my room and grab my backpack, panic filling me. I hate when they fight, but it's different this time: for the first time ever she's not listening to anything Dad has to say, and Mom is known for giving in to whatever he wants.

She's never stormed off like this before, and something in me is telling me not to go with her. I don't have much of a choice, though.

Saint meets me at my door, and I can't hide how worried I am.

"She's making me leave?" I ask him, tears threatening to spill. I don't know what is going to happen, and I'm scared. "Are they breaking up? Oh my God, Saint. I don't want to leave. What if she doesn't let me come back?"

He pulls me into his arms, holding me tight. And when I glance up at him, before I know what's happening, he kisses me. Just a soft, chaste kiss on the lips.

His emotions hit me full force. He doesn't want me to go either. His soft lips leave gentle memories, a first kiss I will never forget, nor regret.

When he pulls back, he rests his forehead on mine. "I'm sure she will just take you to your house until they sort their shit out. You'll be back."

I want to believe him, but there was something in the way Hammer was looking at me that makes me think this is more permanent.

"Sky!" I hear her yell. "Get your ass out here right now. We're leaving!"

"They will make up. This is just a fight that they've taken to the next level," he whispers, cupping my cheek. The look in his eyes contradicts his words. He's worried too.

Shit.

"You're probably right," I tell him, nodding, wishing I could believe him. "Goodbye, Saint."

A muscle tics in his jaw. "I'll see you soon, Sky."

I swallow and follow my mom's screams. Dad hugs me and whispers, "I love you," into my ear before she grabs my arm to drag me into her car.

I stare at the clubhouse as she drives away.

My family.

What has she done?

"He's going to regret dumping me," she says, an evil tone to her threatening words. "Just wait and see. We're going to go home, pack our shit, and then we're leaving. We aren't coming back here, Sky. Ever."

Finally, I let the tears fall.

Chapter Four

"I'll have a cappuccino, please," a man orders. I nod and write it down so I don't forget. One would think I'd be able to remember one drink without problems, but apparently with me and my usual daydreaming, that's not the case. My head is habitually in the clouds, and sometimes I'm not paying attention even when I think I am.

"No problem," I tell him, smiling. "Anything else?"

He shakes his head.

"Won't be long, sir," I say as I move away and head back behind the counter.

I never thought I'd be working at a café full time at twenty-one, but here I am. I took a gap year after high school, which turned into three, and I don't know, I thought at this age I'd be living a little more. Maybe traveling and seeing the world, with a degree behind me. Experiencing life. Instead I'm serving coffee, living with a friend and barely making ends meet. My brother Brooks moved back to the city at the first opportunity, so I'm the only sibling who is still out here in the country, isolated from the rest. But at least my mom is still here. She lives with her new husband, and we catch up once a week or so.

"Sky, can you cover my shift tomorrow?" asks Max, my roommate and coworker, blue eyes pleading. "I know it's your only day off, but I have an audition, and I need to be there."

Max is trying to make it big with his band, and I try to help him out when I can so he doesn't lose his job. He is extremely talented, and I have no doubt that they are going to make it—they just need to get their big break.

I was really looking forward to having my day off, but I can't let him miss this. It's not like I had any great plans, other than sitting on my couch. "Yeah, no problem," I tell him, sighing. "Just remember me when you make it big."

"You know I will," he says, leaning forward and kissing my hair. He steps back and looks above me, spreading his palms out, as if imaging his future. "I'll write a song about you. Sky O'Connor, the only one who had my back *before* I was a millionaire."

"I'll be waiting for it," I reply with a smile, finishing up the cappuccino and taking it over to the customer. I spend the next five hours doing much the same, until it's time for me to head home. I get on my bicycle and ride the fifteen minutes it takes to get to my house, with my red ponytail billowing behind me. Max passes me in his car, his honk scaring the shit out of me. They must have let him finish work early, because I know he wasn't meant to go home for another few hours.

"Race you home!" he calls out, and I roll my eyes at him, but start to pedal faster. There's a shortcut I take that actually makes this a fair race, because even in his car, Max has to go around the longer way. I whizz around a lady walking her dogs, then take the sharp turn to the right, rushing toward our house.

When I get there seconds before him, I jump off my bike and do a little happy dance, shaking my booty and flashing him a smug look. "Ha! You lose! Nice try, though, Max."

He gets out of his car and shakes his head at me, laughing. "Whatever, I let you win!"

I cross my arms and narrow my eyes. "You're such a bad loser."

"You're such a bad winner," he grumbles, grabbing the mail before brushing past me to the door. "I hope no one is dropping in tonight so I can run around naked and drink milk from the carton." His friends have a habit of dropping by unexpectedly, and I've somehow gotten used to it.

I wince at that vision. "Umm, hello? Even if no one else is there, I am. And I'd rather not see you naked. Again."

We've been in our apartment for about a year, and in that time we've both caught each other in some pretty compromising positions. I went from growing up surround by boys to living with one. Platonically. When I was advertising for a roommate to split the rent, I was hoping a nice woman might come along, but nope. Just an up-and-coming rock star waiting for his big break.

I'm just destined to be surrounded by men I have only platonic feelings for.

"Why not? I look good naked," he brags, unlocking the door and gesturing for me to enter. "Ladies first. But wait, you aren't a lady, so…"

He runs in first and I throw my handbag at him. "You're such a jerk! This is why you're single!"

"I'm single because I'm a player!" the idiot calls back

to me, and I can't help but laugh at him. Never a dull moment when Max is around, that's for damn sure. He's like the sixth brother I sure as hell never wanted but got stuck with anyway.

I close the door and head straight for the kitchen, grabbing my bag on the way and placing it down. Picking up the bunch of letters Max threw on the counter, I go through them and pull out the ones for me, walking with them into my bedroom.

"More bills," I grumble, ripping them open. When I come to the last letter, though, it doesn't look like a bill. It's addressed to me in neat handwriting I don't recognize. I open it with caution.

As I read the first line, my heart stops.

Dear Skylar,

    Five years. That's a long time to go without talking to somebody, especially someone who was such a huge part of your life. I hope you are well. I don't even know why I'm writing to you, when you're the last person I'd want to know where I am. But you're also the first person who came to mind when they said I could write snail mail. I can't even remember when I wrote something this long. I think maybe it was on your sixteenth birthday when I wrote out the lyrics to your favorite song in your card. Seems like a lifetime ago.

    The clubhouse was never the same after you left.

    Neither was I.

Saint

Saint.

Saint wrote me a letter. I double-check the envelope,

looking at the return address for the first time, and my eyes grow wide.

Saint, my first ever crush, wrote me a letter.

From prison.

"What have you done?" I whisper to myself, reading the letter once more from the top.

"What's that?" Max asks, as he steps into the doorway of my bedroom.

"Nothing," I say quickly, folding up the letter. I left my heart back in the Knights of Fury clubhouse, with Hammer and Saint, and there hasn't been a day that's gone by that I don't think of them. I was never told what exactly happened that night, other than that Mom and Hammer were done with each other and we needed to get away so we were safe. After we left the clubhouse that night, we drove to our house and she had me and my brother Brooks pack everything. We left a day later and never returned.

Neither Hammer nor Saint have ever reached out to me, until right now.

It's not like it's a surprise for one of the bikers to land themselves in prison, but the thought of Saint being there physically hurts me. It means the world to me to hear from him, but at the same time I do feel a little resentful that it took him being locked up to reach out to me. And another thing... I wonder how he knew where I live. Has he known where I've been this entire time?

I need answers.

"Just more bills," I lie, flashing Max a forced smile, wanting to keep Saint to myself. He rolls his eyes and walks away. I get up to shut my door and walk over to my desk to pull out some paper and a pen from my top drawer. I sit down and start to write.

Saint,
  I'm sorry to hear from you under these circum-
stances. Are you okay? If there is anything I can
do for you, please let me know. You're right, five
years is a long time. I didn't know if I'd ever speak
to you again, but I have thought about you often.
  How is Dad?

I pause, then scrub out the word *Dad*, replacing with
Hammer.

  How is Hammer?
  He always said I would do great things, far away
from the MC, and I guess he was half right. I'm far-
ther away, but I don't know about the doing great
things part. I've put college on hold and am just...
living.
  I guess in prison you'd be doing exactly the same,
just living, pushing through to get to the next day.
  But things will get better, right?
  How much time do you have? I hate the thought
of you behind bars, and I hope that you won't be
in there for too long. I'm here if you need me, and
even though it's probably not much, it's all I can
offer right now.
  And how did you get my address?
  Hang in there, Saint.

Love, Sky
P.S. I still have that sixteenth birthday card.

Chapter Five

Skylar,

You replied. I didn't know if you would or not.

Hammer gave me your address. Just because you left doesn't mean we stopped checking up on you and making sure that you were okay.

I will be in here for about a year, and yes, that time will be spent just living. What's your excuse, though? You should be out there loving life and taking everything it has to offer.

Do that for me, at least, while I'm stuck here eating the worst food I've personally ever tasted. It's worse than that time you were hungry at the clubhouse and I tried to make you spaghetti. Do you remember that? It was awful, but you still ate it without complaining.

I stop reading to remember that moment. I was starving and had just come to the clubhouse after school, but Mom wasn't there and neither was Hammer, so Saint said he'd whip me up something. I remember sitting on the counter, watching him as he boiled pasta and tried to make a sauce from scratch, making do with the lack of ingredients and somehow managing to create a dish.

He'd winced and flashed me an apologetic look as he tasted it, but to me it tasted fine. No, it had tasted great, actually, because he had made it.

> *My cooking skills have improved since then, and*
> *maybe one day I'll be able to prove that to you.*
> *Hammer is fine.*
> *How are you?*
> *Saint*

Sitting back on my couch, beer in hand, I consider his words. Reading that they checked up on me is surprising. Knowing my address and checking up on me are two different things, and not once did they show up at my door and ask me if I was okay. It kind of pisses me off. Why didn't they just reach out to me? Let me know they were still there for me? Anything.

I get up and head to my room, filing the letter away and getting ready to head out to watch Max's band play at one of the local bars. Instead of putting myself out there and loving life, I've just been fumbling along, trying to adult the best I can, but I need to do better.

In an attempt to figure out what I want to do with my life and at the same time stay productive, I've started volunteering at the children's hospital in my spare time. I usually read to them, which doesn't seem like much, but they really enjoy an extra person giving them some attention. Even Max has come in and sung songs for the kids to cheer them up, which has been really rewarding to watch.

I think I've always known that I want to help people in some way or another. I just need to decide what direction I want to go with that.

Now that I am in communication with Saint, he's where my mind tends to be focused, worrying about him and thinking about all the memories I have of the Knights of Fury. The what-ifs also cloud my head. What if my mom and Hammer had never broken up? What if I'd gone back to the city as soon as I turned eighteen? What if I'd kept in touch with Hammer and Saint?

Sliding my feet into my heels, I grab my handbag and head outside, the cool breeze hitting my face. It feels good to get dolled up and I'm excited to see Max play tonight.

After parking my car, I head to the front of the bar and show the bouncer my ID before stepping inside the dimly lit space. The loud music is familiar, chords I've heard Max play over and over from my bedroom. He asked me once if I'd fill in for their lead singer, but I declined. I save my vocals for the shower.

Lucky enough to find a seat by the bar, I glance around at the crowd, smiling as I take in all the people who have come to watch my friends play tonight. I see big things for them in the future.

Max waves to me whilst singing, which has a few women turning around and giving me the evil eye, leaving me feeling amused.

"You here alone?" a gentleman to my right asks me, eyes on me. He's tall and really muscular. He'd be pretty good looking if he got rid of the mustache, but maybe he's just rocking it for Movember. "It's rare to find a woman who won't leave the house without a squad these days."

"A squad?" I repeat, smirking. He mustn't have seen Max's wave, and is probably wondering why I'm sitting here alone. "Well, it's probably smart. Safety in numbers, right? But no, I'm not alone."

And as if any woman in their right mind would admit it even if they were.

He chuckles, sounding truly amused. "That was a terrible opening line, wasn't it?"

"Might need some work," I say, then turn to the bartender to order a drink. I've no interest in this man, or in any other man really. I'm not here to pick up or to be chatted up. I'm just here to watch Max and the rest of the band play and then to go and grab some food with him afterward, as was promised, before heading home and to bed, to sleep next to my pile of clean laundry.

Max tells the crowd they are taking a break for thirty minutes but will be back, and the DJ starts to play some hip-hop music.

"I'll keep that in mind," the guy replies, laughing to himself. He stays silent after that, but I feel his eyes on me.

"Don't even bother with that one," a familiar voice says over my shoulder. "We're pretty sure she's destined for the convent." I turn to Max, who simply grins back at me. "Can't leave you alone for two minutes."

"Well, if it isn't the star himself" I say, turning my stool to face him. "You're amazing up there."

"Thank you," he replies, smiling widely. "It's such a rush. I love being up on the stage."

This is his moment, the first of many, and he deserves to enjoy every second of it.

"And can you believe how many people are here tonight?" he asks me, shaking his head in wonder. "Holy fuck, Sky. This is the best night ever. Come on, drinks are on me."

We have a few celebratory drinks, and I notice the

man who spoke to me before watching me every now and again, but I ignore him, and soon forget about it.

Max finishes up his set, and I stay for the whole thing, loving every moment. Seeing him up there, living his dream, makes me want to chase my own. I want that adrenaline rush, and I want to love what I do every second of every day just like him.

Afterward, he doesn't forget his promise, and we stop for food on the way home.

It's the small things in life.

As I sit down to write Saint, my anger at his and Hammer's silence pour out onto the page.

> *Saint,*
>
> *Of course I'd reply to you. You were all once my family, and that means something to me. I might not be a Knight anymore, or maybe I never was, but I'm loyal like one.*
>
> *What do you mean you all checked up on me?*
>
> *Where were you when I broke my leg at seventeen because I'd gotten drunk for the first time because I was missing my home and looking for an escape? I tried climbing back up to my room to sneak in and fell down the side of the house while trying to scale the wall.*
>
> *You didn't check up on me then.*
>
> *Where were you when, at eighteen, I lost one of the only people I connected to when I moved here? My best friend Shauna died when a drunk driver hit her on the road. It felt like my heart had broken into a million pieces, like I'd lost the sister I never had.*

You didn't check up on me then.
I could go on, but you get the point.
When I left, it felt like I left all of you behind.
Kind of like you all died too.
Sky

I drop the letter off in a mailbox on the way to work, stopping for a few moments on my bicycle. I realize how angry the letter might sound to Saint, and I didn't even know I was angry until now. I guess I feel left behind. Sad. Vulnerable. I know I shouldn't live in the past, but it's hard when I still have so many questions that have been left unanswered after all this time. I didn't realize how much I've bottled up those emotions.

I'm still early when I get to the café, so I take my time in the staff room before clocking in.

"We have the worst crew on today," Max whispers to me when I'm within earshot. "We're basically going to have to be doing the work for everyone."

"You haven't quit yet?" I ask, softly laughing. "After the weekend I thought you'd come in today with your resignation."

"Oh, I'm going on to bigger and better things," he assures me, picking up a tea towel and folding it neatly. "I'm just not going to quit until my bank account reflects my ambition."

"Smart," I agree, nodding. I glance at the roster, and cringe when I read all the names of the young, new staff. "And you're right. We're going to be doing all the work today."

"Told you."

"Lucky you're filled with ambition," I tease.

"Not for this job, I'm not," he grumbles, scrubbing

a hand down his face. "Did you send the letter to your jailbird?"

I stifle a groan. Over food after his concert, I ended up telling Max about Saint, and the letters, and he's pretty much all Max has wanted to discuss ever since.

"Yes, I did," I say, dusting something invisible off my shirt and avoiding eye contact. "And don't make me regret telling you about him."

"No, it was nice to know something personal about you. You're so closed off, Sky. And between us, I kind of thought that maybe you were asexual."

"Just because my door isn't revolving like yours?" I fire back, scowling. "I'm very...uhh...sexual, I'll have you know."

He blinks slowly, then bursts out laughing. "'Uhh sexual'? I said asexual."

"You're an idiot. Besides, even if I were asexual, there is nothing wrong with that," I declare, quieting down when a customer walks in.

Just because I'm not actively having sex doesn't mean that I'm not sexual, or that I couldn't be. I think about sex a lot; I just haven't met that person that I want to experience all those things with. No one has caught my eye or held my attention. I've been on a few dates in my time, but nothing ever came of it. I don't think I've been saving myself for Saint or anything like that, but no one better than him has ever shown up in my life. I've never felt that draw, that pull, that connection like the one I had with him, even if I was only young then.

I'm still young now.

I don't know, maybe I've yet to meet the one, or maybe I've already met him.

I guess only time will tell.

Chapter Six

Skylar,

I hope you are well. I wish we could have this conversation in person. Your mother made it clear we were to have no contact with you, and that if we did, the consequences would fall on you and the MC. We didn't know what to do. She knew a lot about the MC, and we didn't know what she was capable of. At the end of the day, you were her daughter, and she held all the power. I might not have been there to get you through your loss, or be by your side while your leg healed, but you were in my thoughts.

We never forgot you.

Tell me everything else I've missed out on.

I have nothing but time.

Saint

Placing the letter down on my thigh, teeth clenched, my mind roams back to a conversation I had with my mother after she broke up with Hammer. We were on our way to the country, the city becoming farther and farther away in the rearview mirror.

"Did Hammer call you to say bye?" she asks me, tone smug.

"No," I reply, glancing down at my phone, which has zero notifications. *"Did he call you, Mom?"*

"He tried," she says, shrugging. *"But I'm done with him. And if he cared about you like he said he did, he would have contacted you by now. Guess it was all a lie."*

My chest tightens, just like it did back then, at the thought of the man I considered my father, the only father I've ever known, not loving me or fighting to have me in his life. My mother always played the card that Hammer didn't want me without her, and that because they were over, I was no longer of any use to him. Like his love of me was just an extension of her and didn't have its own depth. I'm not going to lie—it cut me, deep.

But what Saint is saying—if it's the truth, which I'm pretty sure it is—means my mother purposely and maliciously lied to me. She made it out like Hammer didn't care about me when that wasn't true. Maybe it was the other way around—maybe he didn't care about her and she couldn't take that. I don't know what to believe anymore.

There's only one person I want to talk to, so I drive straight to her house.

"What are you doing here, Sky?" Mom asks as I get out of my car. She's sitting on the grass, weeding, a large, wide-brimmed hat shielding her from the sun. At fifty-five you'd think life would be slowing down for her, but she still looks and acts like she's not a day over forty. I hope I take after her in this way when I'm older. "Is everything all right?"

It's easy to tell that I rarely drop by unannounced.

Now that I'm here, the words don't seem to come. I kind of don't want to tell her about Saint's letter, because I can only imagine what her reaction will be. She will be angry and want to know every detail, and I haven't seen that side of her in a long time.

"Yeah, everything is fine. Was just passing by so thought I'd drop in and say hello," I lie.

"That's nice of you," she replies, studying me. I don't know how my mother went from leather pants and streaked hair to overalls and gardening, but she did, turning her life around and landing herself a well-off farmer. It's like she changes herself to match whoever she's with, and I don't really think that is a very attractive trait. I hope I never do that. However, I must admit that her new husband is a good influence on her, because she has changed for the better since marrying him.

"What have you and Neville been up to?" I ask her, trying to make conversation.

"Nothing much since we last spoke," she murmurs, removing her hat and wiping the sweat from her brow, her red hair pasted against her forehead. "He's in there making a roast for dinner. Do you want to stay? You look a little thin, Sky. I think you need to eat more."

"Oh, no, it's okay, Mom. I've got food at home waiting for me," I lie.

"If you insist. We spent the day feeding and watering the animals. We have a new foal, if you want to go see her. Neville said you can name her, if you want to."

"I'd love to," I reply earnestly. I think the thing I love the most about visiting here is seeing all their animals. "So, I was thinking about Dad…uh, Hammer today."

I clench my jaw as I wait for her reply.

"He's not your father," she says to me in a gentle tone,

placing her handful of weeds in the bucket then turning to me. "We've had this conversation so many times over the years, Sky. That's not our life anymore, and they are dead to us. We are so much happier out here, and much safer. The best decision I made was moving us away from that life."

"I guess I just don't understand how he could just stop caring about me," I say in a voice much too small. "Did he ever try to contact me, or speak to me? Or even ask how I was?"

"No," she says instantly, jaw tightening. Her green eyes flash and show me a glimpse of the angry old lady she used to be. "He didn't. How many years has it been? Why are you still asking about them? That was another life, and one I don't want to revisit. Hammer wasn't a good man, none of the Knights were, and they don't give two shits about you. You deserve so much better than what they gave you, Sky, and I'm sorry I made you grow up in that environment at all. It was stupid of me. I should have found a nice man like Neville much earlier than I did, instead of getting involved with a…criminal."

Swallowing hard, I nod. This is all I'm ever going to get out of her. She doesn't want to speak about them, and I can't force her. "Yeah, I guess you're right."

Neville comes out, smiling when he sees me. He's a kind man, and I genuinely do like him. I have to give my mother credit—she has great taste. She always finds men who are better than she is.

"Skylar, hello! Will you be joining us for dinner?" he asks.

"No, sorry, Nev. I was just in the area and thought I'd say hello," I say, standing up and brushing the grass off my butt. "And I should probably get going."

The foal will have to wait, because right now all I want to do is get away from my mother. I don't know why I've stayed out in the country with her when I could easily move back to the city and be close to the rest of my siblings and the life I knew before I was dragged out here. I guess I got comfortable and stayed because it was easy. In a messed up way, I also think I see my mom as the only one who has ever stuck by me, so I did the same for her. The MC didn't come for me. My brothers left me. Mom was the only one who didn't leave.

"I'll see you soon," I say, waving quickly before disappearing into my car.

I might not know who Saint is anymore, but I do know who my mother is, and it wouldn't surprise me if she's been lying to me this entire time.

Only one person can clear this up for me, and that's Hammer himself.

Chapter Seven

I don't write back to Saint, because I don't know what to say to him. That it's nice that they all wanted to reach out to me, but no one did? I still have the same number, and there's no excuse that no one called me or sent me a message. It hurts when I think of it like that.

I don't know what to think, and I don't know why they let my mom win so easily. They are a MC, but they let one woman dictate their actions? It makes no sense, and maybe everything Saint is saying is just a bunch of excuses to relieve their guilt. Even with all these thoughts running in my head, I decide to move back to the only place that felt like home. I'm doing it for me, not for them.

I reach out to someone I haven't spoken to in a while: my oldest brother, Logan. When I ask him if I can stay with him until I find my own place in the city, he agrees, and even sounds happy to have me.

After putting in my two weeks' notice at work, I know that I have to tell Max that I'm leaving. To soften the blow, I bake a cheesecake, buy some beer and order pizza. He knows something is up the second he walks in, going by the way he eyes me suspiciously.

"Did someone die?" he asks, frowning. "Ooh, you

baked cheesecake. The last time you baked cheesecake was when Otis got run over. Did our cat die?"

"We don't have another cat," I remind him. "No one has died." I take a deep breath and look him in the eye. "I've decided that I'm going to move back to the city. I'm sorry, and I'm going to miss you so much, but we can all visit each other, and—"

"You're leaving me?" Max asks, brow furrowing. "Why would you want to move when your family is here? I'm here!"

"I just need a change, and I want to go back to college and reconnect with my other family, and… I don't know. I just need a change, okay? You are the only good part about living here. Otherwise, my job is shit—all I do is work and still struggle to make ends meet. My mother only sees me on her terms and we aren't even close no matter how much I try and pretend we are, and…"

And Saint.

And the Knights.

I don't know why, but they are calling me, and I need to find out the truth about everything.

Max sighs and wraps his arm around me. "I'll be doing gigs in the city soon, so it's not the end of the world, but do you know how shitty it's going to be not coming home to you? *You* make this place a home, Sky. You."

Feeling the tears prickling my eyes, I blink rapidly and glance away from them. "I'll still be your home. Just…a movable home."

Max chuckles and pulls me against him. "This better be the best damn cheesecake ever."

Smiling sadly, I grab the plastic plates and hand him

one. "We still have each other." I look him in the eye. "Okay?" He nods.

After he devours the cheesecake, I head into my room to start packing my things. About two hours later, I hear Max call for me in the living room.

"What the hell are you doing?" I ask as I find Max waiting for me with a mischievous grin on his face. That's when I glance down and notice the water gun in his hands. He quickly aims for me and I duck, the stream of water hitting the wall. "Oh my god, we are so not getting our deposit back. Get outside with that!"

I run after him, trying to chase him outside, only to get hit in the face with a stream of water. "I'm going to kill you!"

Max laughs while I run to grab his extra water gun and start filling it up in the sink. "You're not going to live long enough to be famous!"

I hear him laughing harder from outside and decide to follow him out there with my now loaded gun. He has his speaker playing outside, and when I hear what he's listening to, I laugh out loud.

"Oh my god, are you playing your own music for everyone? You're such a lo—"

A bucket of water is tipped over my head.

And then he throws me in the air, over his shoulder, and my damn weapon falls to the ground. I must resemble a raging bull, because I'm fighting to be let go, kicking and screaming until he puts me back down.

"You are going to pay for that!"

"What are you going to do?" he presses, arching his brow. "All talk, Sky. You are all talk. You love it. And you're going to miss the shit out of me while you're back in the fancy city."

His words have never been more true. The truth is that Max is the only thing making me second-guess my decision. He has become my family, and even though he drives me crazy, I'm going to miss him so much. But if I stay here I know I'm not going to be moving forward. I'll be stuck in this rut I seem to have gotten myself in, and I need change.

My heart is telling me to go home.

To where it all started for me.

I throw my hands up in the air, making a promise. "I'm never living with a boy again!"

"I love you, Sky!" Max calls out.

Shit, I love him too.

Goodbye is going to be harder than I thought.

"I don't know why you are going back, Skylar. There is nothing there for you," Mom says with her chin in the air. Strategically, I'd decided to tell her about the move in front of Neville, knowing that she won't react too harshly with him there, wanting to keep her true self hidden.

"All my brothers are there, Mom," I point out, keeping my tone even. "I'm the only one who isn't."

She waves her hand in the air. "You were never even that close with your brothers. Who is going to look after you over there? And you know Neville likes our weekly dinners."

I don't miss how she says *Neville* enjoys the dinners, not her. She's changing, losing the sweet mother façade and returning to a woman I remember well.

Gritting my teeth, I manage to get out, "Well, hopefully that will change now, and I will become closer with them," without losing my temper.

I'm looking forward to reconnecting with them

all again, and there's nothing she can do to stop that. I hardly keep in contact with them anymore. We call each other on our birthdays, and sometimes I see them on Christmas, but that's about it. Like Mom said, we aren't close, and I hate it. And if I'm being honest, part of it is my fault. I always had this irrational sense to stick by my mom. And look what it's given me. Nothing.

She's so against me leaving, but I don't understand why. It's obvious she doesn't want me in contact with any of the Knights, but is that the only reason? It's not like we see each other that often. I don't so much as get a "Happy Birthday" from her unless Neville is there and she wants to put on a show. I visit her because she's my mother, and at the end of the day, I get only one of those. And I respect her because she gave birth to and raised me. She's far from perfect, but yeah, she's all I really have. And she has been much nicer up until I brought up Hammer.

"I'm sure at her age she would much rather be in the city, Georgia," Neville says, rubbing his palm along her shoulder. "Must get boring out here. We don't have many shops, or clubs—"

"Or bikers," Mom mutters under her breath.

"What was that, dear?" Neville asks, none the wiser.

"Oh, nothing, honey. I'm just worried about her being in the city," Mom lies, giving me a filthy look when he's not paying attention.

"Her brothers will look after her," he continues, smiling over at me. "And I'm sure we can come for a visit once she's settled in. I like seeing you every week, but you need to do what is best for you."

"I've already applied for a few jobs, so hopefully I

will have work as soon as I get there. It's a fresh start, and I'm pretty excited about it."

Because my bank balance isn't going to allow for anything else, but also because I'm going to need money to put me through college.

"Do you need any money?" offers Neville, God bless him. "Just for you to get set up. Does Logan have a bed for you? We could pay for you to get one if you like, or anything else you need for your bedroom there."

"That's very kind of you, but I couldn't accept. I will be fine, don't worry about me. Logan said he does have a bed, and I have gas money to get there, so I'm good," I assure him, thanking him again for his kind gesture. It means a lot to me that someone cares, even if it isn't my own mother.

Although the money would be wonderful, I don't feel right taking it from him, or from anyone, for that matter. I made the mistake of asking my mother for financial help right when I graduated high school. I foolishly believed she had a nest egg for me, a college fund. She told me, and I quote, "I raised you for eighteen years and I no longer owe you anything. You're on your own, kid."

I never asked again. That's part of the reason I never enrolled in college too. I had no way to pay for it.

But I'm an adult and I know how to make things work on my own. I need to figure out what I'm going to do with my life. I want more than to serve coffee every day, no offense to people who serve coffee. I just want… more. I can't be relying on anyone else, especially not my mother's new husband, because I have no doubt that she will bring it up and use it against me at some point. Mom has never worked a day in her life and has always lived off men, and I want to make sure I'm never like that. I want to be independent, earn my own money and have a future. It's time I figure out what that future is.

"Are you sure? You know I don't mind—"

"I'm sure she will be fine," Mom cuts him off, shooting me a *you're on your own now* look. "She's an independent woman, aren't you, Skylar?" she asks, as if she can read my mind.

"I like to think so," I reply, squaring my shoulders.

The second Neville disappears into the kitchen to get us some coffee, Mom is on me. "You came here the other day bringing up Hammer, and now you're telling me you're moving back there? If this has anything to do with him, you're more of a foolish girl than I thought. If you think you can just walk into that clubhouse…he will kill you, Skylar."

Hammer would never hurt me, and I know that for a fact. She let that man raise me, but the second they broke up he's bad news? It makes no sense, and I don't really believe anything she says anymore.

"I never said anything about walking into that clubhouse or even seeing them," I say. "I know I'm not one of them anymore, Mom. I want to make something of myself, and here I'm just wasting away."

"The only thing you want to make of yourself is some biker's slut. If you think Saint still even remembers who you are, you have another thing coming," she whisper-yells.

My jaw drops.

One, because I never knew that she knew I had a thing for Saint, and two, because how dare she say that to me? She couldn't possibly be more hypocritical if she tried.

"A biker's slut? You mean what you were?" I fire back, unable to contain my anger any longer. She was an old lady, so I know it's not exactly true, but she was still with a biker and lived that lifestyle, so she can't talk. "Bit hypocritical of you, isn't it? I wouldn't have even known that life if it wasn't for you, so don't act like any of this is my fault. Perhaps if you told me who my real father was I wouldn't have to go around looking for father figures. Or is it that you don't even know, mother dearest?"

With that, I stand and head to the kitchen to tell Neville I have to leave early. I give him a hug and tell him thank you for always being so kind to me, and then get in my car and drive back home.

Home. Or at least my home for the next few days.

Can I still call it that?

Chapter Eight

Happiness is wind in my hair and a road trip leading to a fresh start. Music pumping, I try to push away the sadness at saying goodbye to Max, and leaving him standing outside watching my car disappear down the road. I know I'll see him again, but it's the end of an era, and I can't pretend that it's not.

I'm not sure how I'm going to navigate life without him, but I'm going to find out.

I finally answered Saint's letter, telling him about the move and not to reply to my old address anymore. I didn't give away too much information, but I wanted him to know that I could no longer be reached there. I guess I did want him to know I'll be closer to him too, even if I don't know what that is going to mean just yet.

I see a familiar face when I stop for gas, the man with the mustache who tried to talk to me at the bar. He pretends like he doesn't notice me, and I'm more than okay with that, so I too ignore him, pay for my gas and leave.

I arrive at Logan's a few hours later. I'm ashamed to admit I've been to his house only once before, and that was when we all had Christmas together about two years ago. His wife, Sabrina, seemed nice enough the one time I met her, and I hope that she doesn't mind that I'm going to be staying here for a while. Knocking on the door, suitcase dragging behind me, I take a deep breath and wait as I hear the door opening.

"Sky, you made it," Logan says, green eyes smiling. He pulls me in for an awkward hug, then steps back and gestures for me to enter. "Come in."

"Thanks, Logan," I reply, stepping through with my suitcase.

"Here, let me take that for you."

"Thanks. Where's Sabrina?" I ask, following behind him into the kitchen.

"She's at work. Do you want something to eat or drink? Or should I show you your room first?" he asks, running his hand through his brown hair, looking a little unsure.

"I ate on the way, so I'm okay."

"Room it is," he murmurs, gesturing upstairs. "You have the whole upstairs area to yourself."

"Thanks for letting me stay here, Logan," I say as he carries my suitcase up the stairs. "I know we haven't spoken much recently, and—"

"We're still family, Sky," he says, cutting me off. "And if you need me, I'm here for you. All right?"

"All right, thanks," I say softly, not expecting such kind words from him.

He shows me my bedroom, which is larger than I had anticipated, with a queen-sized bed and walk-in closet for my clothes. It even has a bathroom attached.

"I can't remember the last time I didn't have to share a bathroom," I admit, smiling over at him. "This is amazing, Logan."

"Good thing I bought a four-bedroom house, right?" He grins, glancing around. "We planned it so we wouldn't have to move when we had kids, but..." He trails off, shrugging. Mom had mentioned to me that Logan and Sabrina were trying to conceive, but were having no luck. He hasn't said anything to me about it personally, though, so I decide not to comment. If he wants to talk to me about it, that's up to him.

"Hopefully I will find a job this week and be out of your hair before you know it."

"There's no rush," he quickly says, placing his hands in his pockets. "It's been a while since I've gotten to spend some time with you, especially with Mom not around. It will be nice. I told Brooks and Seth to come over for dinner this weekend, so it will be a mini-sibling reunion. Shame the rest of them aren't around."

Smith and Axel are currently overseas, traveling and working together around the world. Last I heard they were in Northern Ireland. They both used to have corporate jobs, but one day they packed up and left, starting their own travel blog, which is increasing in popularity every day.

"Yeah, but that still sounds really nice, actually," I say, sitting down on the bed. "It's been a while since we've been together. And whenever Smith and Axel get home, I'll be around to catch up with them properly." I haven't seen them all since the last Christmas we spent together, which was two years ago.

He nods. "It has. Too long. Well, Sabrina changed the sheets for you and put a fresh towel in the bathroom. Anything else you need, let me know. Make yourself feel at home."

Before he heads back downstairs, I stand up, step toward him and give him a big hug.

A proper hug.

One with my arms around his waist, my cheek pressed against him, and my eyes closed.

He didn't have to look after me like this, but I'm grateful that he is.

He squeezes me back, then steps away, flashing me a sheepish smile.

"Thank you," I say once more.

"Don't mention it, baby sis," he replies, then disappears.

Lying back on my new bed, I stare up at the ceiling and smile.

"Why aren't you in the kitchen cooking?" Brooks asks me that weekend, smirking. "Is Sabrina in there doing all the work?"

"No, actually, Logan is cooking. Sabrina and I did the dessert, though. Also, stop being a pig—it's 2019," I tell him, frowning. "Let me guess, you're still single?"

Brooks and I still rub each other the wrong way, but in a sibling way. We are only a year apart, so you'd think we'd get on better, but nope. Fire and ice.

I'm fiery, and he's cold. But I still love him.

"Yeah, he is," Seth laughs, taking his own cap off then resettling it back on his head. "I've never even seen him with a girlfriend."

"The type of women I like aren't the ones you bring home," Brooks adds, raising his brows suggestively. He then looks around the room. "And I don't see your woman here anyway, Seth. Where is she?"

"At work," Seth replies, returning his gaze to the TV and then toward me. "You never told us why you suddenly decided to move here, not that we aren't happy you're close to us now. Mom driving you crazy?"

Now all eyes are suddenly on me.

"Okay, well, there was nothing there for me in the country. I want to make a career for myself, and I want a change. I only had Mom there and it's not like I was spending more than an hour a week with her, so..." I trail off, shifting in my seat.

"Are you going to go to college?" Seth asks, pushing his glasses back up on his nose. He's the only one of my brothers who has a degree, so of course it's him asking me that. "You're a smart girl, Sky. You could do anything you want. Didn't you want to be a vet growing up?"

I nod. "I did, yeah."

"So why don't you make it happen?" he asks, studying me. "I told you that working in that café was a waste of your time."

"Having money to eat and pay rent was kind of necessary, Seth," I tell him, rolling my eyes. "And I didn't come here for an interrogation, okay? I am going to go to college. I want to do something where I can help people and actually make a difference."

"Leave her alone," Logan chastises, and it feels so good to finally have someone on my side for once. "She's here, and that's all that matters right now. She's trying to do something new. She's never even been away from Mom before, so let's cut her some slack, all right?"

"Excuse me, you guys are acting like I've been living with Mom all of this time when I haven't. I've just been in the same town as her. She hasn't been supporting me, financially or otherwise, for a long time. Just because you guys all bailed long before I was of legal age doesn't make my situation any different," I tell him, frowning. "So don't give me any shit just because I'm a girl and the youngest."

They all stay silent for a few seconds, and then

Brooks says, "Is it too early to crack open that bottle of vodka I bought?"

"You only brought one?" I ask, lip twitching, glancing at each of my brothers' faces.

He throws his head back and laughs, then stands up and heads to the front door to go to his car, I'm assuming. "This is an O'Connor gathering. Of course I didn't just bring one bottle. I'll go and get my stash."

"He has a bottle shop in his car?" Seth asks, looking a mixture of impressed and horrified.

"Georgia O'Connor raised him. Of course he does," Logan mutters.

I don't miss all the digs made at Mom, but no one says anything directly to me, and I'm not sure how they feel about her.

However, I feel like there's something I'm missing, and I'm going to find out what it is.

Chapter Nine

"Well, that's what Hammer said," Seth says to Brooks, making my ears prick up.

"You've spoken to Hammer?" I ask him, sitting down next to him on the couch and looking him in the eye. We've all been vegging out in the living room, catching up on life, eating and watching movies. I forgot how much I love hanging out with all of them. "How is he?"

"Yeah, he checks in on us every now and again," Seth says, biting the inside of his lip. "Makes sure we aren't in any trouble. Not that we tell Mom that. She'd kill us if she knew."

So Saint was right. Mom didn't want Hammer to have anything to do with us, not the other way around.

"She told me that he doesn't care about any of us, and that he never once tried to make contact," I say, glancing between them.

"That's bullshit. He's always asking how you are," Seth admits, eyes softening on me.

"How come no one told me about this?"

"I don't know. You were over there with Mom, and we didn't know what you were thinking, or if she had gotten into your head about Hammer."

"Mom never wanted to give up her control of you,

Sky," Brooks adds, shrugging. "Trust me, it was just easier to stay away from all of that."

"You're an asshole," I tell him, digging my fingers into my palm. "You all had some kind of brotherhood going on and I was left in the dark, being told that Hammer and the MC washed their hands of me the same time they did Mom."

"You were only sixteen when you left, Sky," Logan adds, sitting down and joining the conversation. "We didn't want you dragged into some drama, and thought maybe it was best that you were away from it all out there in the country. Neville is a sweet guy, and Mom has been playing nice because of him, so we figured we'd leave it be."

"Why did you want nothing to do with the MC?" I ask him, something I have always wondered.

Logan winces and rubs the back of his neck. "You know that I never felt at home there. I remember walking into the clubhouse one time with Mom. I was like seventeen, but we were a little early and I saw something I wasn't meant to." He shakes his head, as if trying to forget the memory. "And Mom acted like it was fucking normal, when it wasn't. I just remember thinking, what the fuck am I doing here? It wasn't the life I wanted, and I never really clicked with any of the men. I remember you as a kid, coming home after you got into a fight, because the other kids judged you because of your parents. I didn't like that. I don't know. It was just never my home, Sky. Ever. I know it was yours, and that's okay, but it wasn't for me. Hammer was a different man to you than he was to the rest of us. He saw you as his daughter, but we weren't his sons. We never called him Dad, and he never did for us the things he did for you."

"I never thought of it that way," I whisper, not knowing what to say. He's right, they never did call Hammer "Dad," and I guess it's because they're older and remember their own father. Hammer obviously cared about them all, I don't doubt that for a second, but maybe he didn't have the same bond with them that he did with me. I suddenly feel a little sad about that. We should have all been treated equally no matter what. We should have always stuck together, but we didn't.

"And we knew when you were old enough you'd get sick of Mom's shit," Brooks says, smirking. "Took a bit longer than we thought, but that's okay."

"How about a fucking invitation or something? I had no idea if I was even welcome here. Our family isn't exactly the Brady Bunch, and nothing was the same after I moved away. You barely kept in touch with me, and now I feel like the baby, the lone black sheep or something," I grumble, crossing my arms.

"Ah, come on, don't pout," Seth grumbles in return, reaching out and touching my shoulder. "We should have put in more effort to keep in contact with you. It was just hard, because then we had to deal with Mom, and that's not always easy. Especially when it comes to you."

"What does that even mean? Especially when it comes to me?" I ask him.

He glances away, looking to Logan for some help.

"Mom's just really weird when it comes to you," Logan admits, a look of sadness passing in his gaze. "It's like if we ask about you, or show interest in you, she doesn't like it and wants to bring the attention back to her. I don't know…it's almost like she sees you as competition. And I know this isn't a really nice thing to say or whatever, but that's just how I see it. I feel like she's jealous of you, and always has been. She was the queen, surrounded by all these boys doting on her, and then you came along. The last sibling, beautiful, smart. We all fell in love with you. Including Hammer and his men. And she didn't like that."

Eyes wide, I sit back in my chair and take a deep breath. I've never thought about this from that perspective before. I knew I wasn't Mom's favorite, but it never crossed my mind that she was jealous of me.

Why would she be? It's true that the men in the MC tended to spoil me growing up, and my brothers always cared for me. Could it be possible that my own mother didn't like that? The thought is foreign to me. What kind of mother feels that way about her only daughter?

"I don't even know what to say right now…" I glance around at my brothers, taking them each in individually. Brooks looks more like me, with his red hair and green eyes, but Seth and Logan have brown hair and brown eyes like their dad.

"Which is why we never said anything," Logan continues, running his hand through his dark brown hair. "How do you tell your little sister something like that? It's complicated, makes no sense and is kind of twisted."

"It's not like Mom was mean to you or anything," Brooks adds in, shrugging. "She just…is more of a boys' mom."

I roll my eyes at him. "Seriously? All of you seem to think she's crazy, so she can't have been that great of a mother to all of you, either."

"She *is* crazy," Logan agrees, making the others chuckle. "She has her good moments. She's not evil. She just has a very…unpredictable side to her. She's manipulative and can be quite conniving when she needs to be."

"Understatement," Seth adds, standing behind me and resting his hands on my shoulders. "You're out of her grasp now, that's all that matters. And if you want to go and see Hammer, you can. She doesn't control your life anymore."

"Have any of you seen or spoken to Saint?" I dare ask. I have no idea if they knew about my crush on him or not.

"Nope," Logan replies, shaking his head. "We've only spoken to Hammer. Why? Still have that stupid-ass crush on him?"

I'll take that as confirmation that they knew.

"I have no idea what crush you're talking about, but yes, Saint was a big part of my life once upon a time," I admit, accepting the ice-cold glass of vodka and lemonade that Seth passes my way. "Thank you, Seth. So what else have I missed out on while I've been segregated?"

"Nothing much on my end," Brooks answers first, downing his glass then giving me his attention. "Still working at the sandalwood factory."

We chat for a bit, and then we have dinner, a lasagna and salad that Logan made for us. Sabrina comes back from work just in time to have some of the dessert we both made earlier today, chocolate cheesecake and strawberries, before the boys start heading home. It's been so long since I felt like I could open up and be close to my brothers, like when we were little, but after tonight I realize how much I've missed them all. Even Brooks, who is generally a total asshole.

I already feel like I've made the right choice by moving here.

There's no going back now.

Saint,

Sorry it's been so long since I've written to you. I've been settling in at Logan's house and found a new job at a bar, so I've been pretty busy. I've been looking at different colleges too, trying to figure out what my passion is and what I'm meant to do.

How are you doing? I've been thinking about going to visit Hammer, but I'm not sure if I should call him or just show up. Am I even welcome there anymore? Maybe calling would be safer. I don't really know what to expect, but I do want to see him, and I do want some answers. How would you feel about me coming to visit you?
Sky

I write this letter, but then decide not to send it. Some things are just better said face-to-face.

I'm going to go see Hammer.

And then I'm going to go and see Saint.

Feeling extremely nervous, I step onto the Knights of Fury MC turf. The last time I was here I was being dragged away and put into Mom's car, which was five years ago. So much has changed since then, but the club-house building remains exactly the same, the brown brick, the rickety metal fence and the worn wooden door. There's a few bikes out front, making me pause for a moment as I scope them out, trying to see if I remember any of them but coming up short.

Slowly, my white canvas shoes take me to the entrance. I knock once, and then twice, louder, when no one answers the first time.

"Is that someone knocking?" I hear a masculine voice

ask. "Jesus Christ. Those knocks were too polite to be the cops. Who the fuck could it be?"

I don't know if anyone has even knocked on this door, other than police, because normally everyone just walks in like they own the place. However, I don't really feel comfortable doing that, especially when I don't even know if Hammer is in there.

"I hope it's someone selling chocolate or candy," another voice adds, just before the door opens, and I see Renny, aka Renegade, and Temper standing in front of me. While I wasn't that close with Renny growing up, Temper was one of my favorite bikers. The man has a heart of gold for the select few he lets in. For everyone else, though…if Temper doesn't like you, you should get the fuck out of Dodge.

"Sky?" Temper asks, brow furrowing. "Is that you? Holy fuck, it is! What the fuck happened to you? You grew up on me."

He opens his arms, and I run into them. "And you grew old on me, Temper."

"Only you can get away with saying shit like that, trouble," he mutters, voice husky. "What in hell are you doing here? You're the last person I thought to see on the other side of this door."

I let go of him and turn to Renny, offering him a shy smile. "Renny."

"Sky," he replies, stroking my hair. "Hammer is going to be fuckin' happy to see you."

Relief fills me, and my shoulders release all of their tension. "Is he here?"

Temper nods and pulls me gently by the wrist. "Come on."

He leads me through the house and outside to the

yard, and that's where I see him on a chair, smoke in hand, staring out at the sky.

"Hey, Prez, look who the cat dragged in," Renny calls out ahead of us.

Hammer doesn't even turn around. "If it has tits I'm not in the mood," he calls out, tone irritated.

"I mean, she does have them, but I'm not gonna look at them if I wanna live to tell the story," Renny says, chuckling deeply.

This seems to get Hammer's attention. His slow head turn has my nerves racing. He looks the same. A little grayer, a few more wrinkles around his eyes, but he's exactly how I remembered him.

Sky? he mouths, shaking his head slightly, as if to clear it. He looks surprised, shocked...but also happy. Standing, he opens his arms and smiles widely, approaching me. When he reaches me, he hugs me so tightly that all of the pieces fit back together.

Home.

I'm home. I'm safe.

"Dad?" I whisper, feeling emotional, tears prickling at the back of my eyes. I bury my face into his worn brown leather jacket and just hold on to him for dear life.

He kisses the top of my head. "I knew you'd come back."

Lifting my face up, looking him in the eyes, I say, "Did you? Because I didn't."

Sadness fills his brown gaze. "I hoped that you would. Does your mother know that you are here?"

I shake my head. "No, and I'm not going to tell her. My brothers told me what happened. I know she didn't want any of us to have any contact."

Which is quite the understatement. Mom is the one

who took me away from Hammer. She didn't want me to have a relationship with him because she no longer did.

I pull back from him and wipe my eyes with my palms. "Is someone cutting onions?"

They must be. I'm sure of it. I'm not much of a crier, and I'm the type who tends to bury her emotions as much as she can. Suffer in silence, that's my motto.

"I've missed you," I admit.

The man standing before me is the only parent who has ever shown me love, the only one who made me feel like I'm not a failure. Up until we left, Hammer had done nothing but love, support and be there for me, and even though it's been years, all of those feelings and emotions come back. They say you never remember what a person says, you remember only how they made you feel, and right now I feel loved and cherished, and it's all coming back like it was yesterday.

This man took me to the hospital when I broke my arm.

He made me soup when I was sick.

He threatened the parents of the boy who was mean to me in fifth grade.

Through all the years he was the one who got me through everything, and now I have him back.

"I've missed you too, Sky," he replies, cupping my face and smiling down at me. "Welcome home."

Chapter Ten

The next voice I hear is one I didn't expect.

"Skylar?"

I look around Hammer to see Saint himself, standing at the door. He's dressed in a pair of low-slung jeans and he's not wearing a shirt. My eyes linger on his body, one that was once bare but now is covered in tattoos and muscles, and I don't know where to look right now. He's beautiful. He seems older, more mature, and there's a weariness in his eyes that wasn't there before.

"What are you doing here?" I ask him, lost for words.

I thought I'd have a little time to prepare myself before seeing him, and when I did it was going to be at the prison, so this whole meeting has caught me off guard. I'm still drawn to him like no other, and I can't seem to look away from him. It's been so long since I laid eyes on that face and heard that voice, and now that he's finally in front of me I don't really know what to say or do. The last time we saw each other we were friends and I was a child. Yes, I was sixteen, but it was a schoolgirl crush. But now…seeing him as an adult woman has me feeling all sorts of things I don't know if I'm supposed to feel. I'm still very much attracted to him. Is this normal?

As I study him, I can see he's looking at me in that

same inscrutable way he always did. But this time, there is something else. It's like he's seeing me for the first time. He's never looked at me this way before.

"I could say the same about you," he murmurs, stepping toward me.

Hammer backs away and lets us have our moment, and when Saint's arms come around me, his warm skin pressing against me, I don't have words to express how I'm feeling. I've thought about this moment for so long, but it's so much more than I ever thought it was going to be.

"They let you out early?" I surmise, looking up at him. "I didn't expect to see you here, that's for sure."

He nods. "Yeah, early release. Long story."

"I have all the time in the world to hear about it," I reply with an arched brow.

Lip twitching, he smiles down at me. "I can't believe you're standing here right now. When you never wrote back to me, I just thought that you'd given up."

Staring at the tattoo on his chest, a knight with a grim reaper ax, I say, "Nope. I was actually going to visit you at the prison next, after I got the details from Hammer, but looks like you beat me to it. I'm glad you're back home; I didn't like the thought of you locked up."

"I didn't like the thought of it either," he replies, lip twitching. "And I've never been happier to be home than I am in this moment. You're a sight for sore eyes, Skylar. I feel like I'm fucking dreaming or something."

I think that's a good thing.

"I feel like this is a cause for celebration," I hear Renny mutter to Temper. "Is she old enough to finally attend one of our parties?"

"We don't want to scare her off just yet," Hammer mutters in a dry tone. "She just got here."

"Think the last thing she needs is to be around half-naked women and lots of bikers, Renny," Temper replies, smirking. He slaps him on the back. "But if you need that, we can make it happen."

"Excellent," Renny says, rubbing his hands together in anticipation. "It's been a while."

Saint touches my cheek, bringing my attention back to him. "Come on, let's go sit inside. I'll make you a coffee, or see if we have anything to eat in the fridge."

"Good luck," Hammer calls out, laughing softly. The other men don't follow us, which I appreciate, giving me that little alone time with Saint.

"There used to always be food here," I point out, remembering the days I'd open the cupboards and fridge and think I'd won the lottery.

"There used to be women around here," Saint replies, opening the door for me. "It's just us now, and well. The place has a more bachelor vibe to it. None of us have old ladies, and the older members don't live here anymore—they're with their families—so it's just about ten of us now."

"Bachelors don't need to eat?" I tease, heading for the kitchen with him at my heel. "And I highly doubt it that there aren't any women here."

As much as I don't want to think of it in regards to Saint, I know that the Knights are notorious ladies' men. I've seen it with my own eyes, even if I wasn't allowed to officially attend any of their club parties, and I heard the rumors about Saint and how he got his name. He just has this allure to him; I don't think he needs to even try with women—they just fall at his feet.

It sucks to think that I also might be in that same category, but I like to think that I'm different, because we also have a genuine friendship, or at least we had one. I don't know where we stand now, but we're both here right now and that means something. He reached out to me, and now I've found my way back. If Saint didn't want anything to do with me romantically, I'd happily still be in his life as a friend, and I truly do mean that. I want to see him happy no matter what, and if that's not with me then I'd accept that.

"None that stay around and feed us," Saint replies, opening the fridge and scanning its contents. "If I knew you were coming, I would have run to the store. How about I order us all pizza or something?"

He turns the kettle on, then sits down at the table, so I do the same. "I'm fine, Saint," I tell him, grinning.

I'm too excited to eat, nerves and happiness mixing together into a giddiness.

"I can't stop looking at you," he blurts out, and then ducks his head. "You're so different since the last time I saw you."

"Good different?" I ask, wishing that I knew what he was thinking.

"Yeah." He smiles and just stares at me, our eyes locking. After a while, he shakes himself out of a daze. "Tell me how you ended up here, because I bet it's a fuckin' story."

I tell him about my conversation with Mom, my decision to move and the sadness at leaving my roommate. We talk about my brothers and how I decided I was just going to show up and hope for the best.

Blue eyes watch me as he listens intently and then

says, "Well, there you go. Even I had no idea Hammer was checking in with your brothers."

"Glad someone else was in the dark with me."

A man steps into the kitchen, and I recognize him instantly. "What the fuck?"

He waves, a sheepish grin on his face. "I'm Dee."

"Dee?" I ask, confused. "You're a member? Why the fuck were you following me?"

Did Hammer ask him to watch me?

"I'm a prospect," he admits, looking to Saint to explain the situation, I guess.

"He was checking up on you to make sure you were all right," he explains, wincing and running a hand through his dark hair. It's a little shorter than I remember it. "I know it sounds bad, but like you said in your letter, we aren't there with you, so we wanted to make sure you were okay, and to do that we needed eyes on you."

"You or Hammer could have come yourselves!" I point out, scowling. "Or Temper. Renny. Any of you. And you could have come and actually said hello to me."

"We couldn't send someone your mother was going to recognize—that would bring a hell of a lot of drama we don't need. So we sent someone she wouldn't know," he explains, shrugging like it makes perfect sense to him. If he wasn't sitting here all sexy, shirtless, and if it hadn't been so long since I'd seen him, I might have slapped him.

"So you sent some guy to come and talk to me in a bar?" I mutter to myself, shaking my head. "Next time a phone call will suffice, Saint."

He throws Dee a look that says *bye* then turns back to me. "I'm seeing you for the first time in five years and you want to fight?"

"How did I know you were going to play that card?" I groan, quieting when he reaches out and touches my arm.

"Let me get used to seeing you all grown up before you rip into me, all right?" he asks, flashing me a charming smile. He then stands to make our coffee. "Do you have any plans tonight?"

"No. I have to work tomorrow, but that's about it."

"Where are you working?" he asks, sounding confused. "More like *why* are you working?"

"You know, to do things like eat," I say slowly, arching my brow. "And buy things. I only just started at this new bar, but it's a pretty cool place."

Saint, mug in hand, comes over and places it on the table. "What did you do with the money Hammer gave you? Are you saving it? I thought you'd go to college and just live off that so you didn't have to worry about anything else except your studies."

Confusions hits me. I dare to ask, "What money?"

Saint's brows draw together, and concern fills those blue eyes. "The college fund Hammer set up for you. He's been putting money into it ever since you came into his life."

College fund? I've never heard the words *college fund* in relation to me. My mother never gave me a cent, and always made me work for anything that I wanted. "I didn't get any money, Saint. Mom never told me that there was any money."

"Nothing?" he asks, jaw going tense.

I shake my head. "No, nothing."

"That fucking bitch," he mutters, slamming his hands down on the table, making his coffee drip down the mug. "Hammer!" he calls out. Studying me, he murmurs, "Stay here a second," then disappears outside.

I can hear the two of them yelling before they come reappear in the kitchen. "Georgia didn't give you any of that money?" Hammer asks me, searching my eyes.

I shake my head. "No, nothing. I had no idea I had any kind of savings anywhere. I've always just lived paycheck to paycheck." Not a luxurious life, but I've always gotten by.

"There was a hundred thousand dollars in that account for you," he growls, fist clenching. "I made it so you could access it when you turned eighteen."

Wow, that's a lot of money. A hundred thousand?

Wrapping my arms around myself, I don't know what else to say. This woman I thought I could trust, even if we weren't as close as some kids are with their mothers, has lied to me over and over. And now she's had money that was supposed to be mine while she knew I struggled to pay my bills? And never told me about it? I'm speechless.

"Guess she thought Sky would never speak to us again, so she'd never find out about the money," Saint says, shaking his head. "The nerve of her, honestly. That money was for Skylar's future!"

"I asked her for some money once," I say in a whisper, remembering the day so clearly. "She told me that she was done taking care of me and I was on my own. That she had five other children, and how could I expect there to be anything left for myself? That I was ungrateful. It's why I didn't go to college right away…"

My brain cannot process this. I cannot understand how she can lie to me and make me feel that it was my fault. This can't be true.

"Maybe there is more to the story. Maybe she still has it and was waiting to give it to me," I say, but the words sound stupid even to my own ears. It's just embarrassing that my own mother would manipulate me and use me so easily, and I was none the wiser, visiting with her every week, playing my role as the good daughter, the only child she had close by to her.

The men don't even bother with a response, and I don't need one, because I know the words I just spoke are lies. I take a deep breath. "It's fine. Thank you for thinking of me, Hammer. I think it's the nicest thing anyone has done for me."

Swallowing hard, I look down at my hands.

Don't cry.

Don't cry.

Don't cry.

Strong arms come around me. "I'll fix this for you."

Glancing up, I smile at my dad.

Saint steps closer, touching my shoulder, silently giving him his strength. "No one is going to hurt you anymore, Sky. We've got you now."

The tears fall.

Chapter Eleven

"Safe to say today has been an emotional day," I state, sighing heavily. I must look like crap, after crying and rubbing my face, I imagine my mascara must be everywhere, and I'm feeling completely overwhelmed. Seeing Hammer and finding out my own mother doesn't have my best interests at heart has taken its toll on me. I mean, I shouldn't be surprised, but that doesn't mean that the reality of it doesn't hurt.

And then there's Saint.

I want to hold him, to be held by him, but with Hammer here it's kind of awkward, and just because we've finally reconnected doesn't mean we are anything. Yeah, he wants to do dinner tonight, but that could just be to catch up. It's not like he's ever said he had any feelings for me other than friendship. Oh god. What if he still thinks of me as a little sister?

My life is a fucking mess, and I almost feel like I need to go home and crawl into bed right now to process everything.

"Been a bit of a surprise for us all," Hammer mutters, then smiles at me with gentle eyes. "Don't worry about anything, Sky."

He says that, but I still have so many questions. Is now the time to bring them up or should I wait?

"Why didn't you fight for me?" I blurt out, unable to keep myself quiet. "With your reaction today, it's like you missed me and wanted me to come back here. So why didn't you fight for me? Call me? Visit me? Send me a fucking message? Something. Anything?"

"It's complicated," he says, sharing a look with Saint, who appears to want to make a quick exit from this conversation. "Your mom held all the power with you, Sky. You were *her* daughter, no matter how much she didn't deserve you—"

"I was your daughter too," I cut him off. "I *am* your daughter. Or don't you feel that way anymore?"

"Of course I do," he says quickly.

"Then don't play that card. You not being my biological father doesn't mean anything to me," I say, looking him in the eye. "I know there's something you aren't telling me. I'm not stupid. There's no way in hell the whole MC is so scared of Georgia O'Connor that they never want to go up against her. Sending me a message or calling me wouldn't have upset anyone except her. So what does she have on you?"

That has to be the only reason: Mom must have blackmailed them with something. It's that or they simply didn't care enough about me and gave up. There's no other explanation.

Hammer rubs the back of his neck. "Fucking hell, Skylar. There's some things that are better left unsaid, and this is one of them. Don't push this, because you won't like the truth, and I won't be able to fucking sleep at night knowing that you know. So please, let it be. I'm so fucking happy to have you back—don't make me break your heart on the same day."

He cups my cheek, smiles sadly, then leaves the room.

"He's really going to say all that and then bail?" I ask Saint, shaking my head. "What could possibly break my heart any more than it's already been broken?"

Saint wraps his arms around me. "Your mom and Hammer had a complicated relationship, as I'm sure you remember. They hated each other half the time and were obsessed with each other the other half. It was unhealthy. Who knows what went on between them that we don't know about?"

I breathe easier knowing Saint has been left in the dark with me. "I do remember."

Unhealthy is the right word. The two of them had a passionate, yet volatile relationship, one with a lot of drama. I've blocked out most of it and pretended it was normal, but it wasn't. Hammer was always the stable parent in my life, and considering he's the president of an MC, that's saying something. We did have plenty of good times as a family, though, and they are what I try to remember.

Saint holds me tighter.

After having not seen him for so long, I can feel that we are still connected.

But in what way is to be determined.

Saint and I head out to dinner, but I requested something low-key and casual, so we decide on a little Indian place that we used to all eat from back in the day.

"Nice to see that some things around here don't change," I say as we walk inside, smiling at the familiar décor. Saint pulls out my chair, waiting for me to be seated before doing the same. Looking over the small table at him, I start feeling a little shy. It's just us now, no distractions, and it feels more intimate than I imagined it would be.

"Your hair is so long now," he muses, staring at it. "It's beautiful."

"Thank you," I say, feeling myself blush a little. "Yours is just how I remember it, just a little shorter, though."

He runs his hand through his thick, dark hair. "Yeah, I cut it but it grew back. It grows fast. Do you like it like this, or think I should get rid of it?"

"I like it," I say, wanting to run my own fingers through it. "I don't think many men can pull it off, but it suits you. It always has."

Between all the dark hair, piercing blue eyes and his body, I must say he has a lot going for him, and I know that there's no way in hell that I'm the only one who notices that.

"Okay, I'll keep it then," he says with a wolfish grin, picking up the menu in front of him.

"So when did you get out exactly?" I ask.

"Two days ago," he replies. "So good timing on your behalf."

The waitress comes over, and we order our drinks and meals.

"How's it been moving in with Logan?" he asks me, changing the subject away from him. "You know you can always move into the clubhouse with us."

"Thanks for the offer," I say, grinning. "But it's pretty sweet at Logan's, and it's nice to have my own space. He and Sabrina have given me their entire upstairs—it's a really cool setup. Because of our age difference, I never

really got a chance to get to know him. I feel like this is
my second chance to get to know my brothers in a different way. I saw Seth and Brooks as well. It's great to
be surrounded by family."

"I'm glad you have them, then," he replies, studying
me. I notice a freckle on his olive skin, on his left cheek,
one that wasn't there before.

"Yeah. I do miss my best friend and old roommate,
though…"

Saint shakes his head. "You couldn't go live with a
bunch of girls, could you?" he grumbles, lip twitching.
"It had to be with a dude, and one who is a rock star."

"How'd you know that?" I ask, wondering how he
knew about Max. But then I remember my stalker. "Did
Dee tell you?" I roll my eyes. "Max is family to me.
There is nothing between us but friendship."

He nods, and I take a moment to bask in the fact that
I'm sitting here. With Saint.

"You're the same, but different," I announce, looking
away from his intense blue gaze. "Like, I know you, but
at the same time I don't anymore. I've missed out on so
much, Saint. You need to catch me up."

We're both different, older people now, and hopefully
more mature. I want to know everything I've missed
out on, and what has happened in his life in the last
few years.

"I feel the same way about you," he admits. "You
were just a girl back then."

"And now?"

"And now you're a woman," he replies, lip twitching.
"Those few years were good to you."

"Are you saying I was ugly back then?" I joke, laughing.

"No," he replies, laughing with me. "But you were

young, Sky. I only saw you as a girl, because that's what you were. We were friends."

"I know," I admit. "Although I did have a bit of a crush on you."

"I know," he replies, grinning. "But you know how difficult a position it put me in. I had to balance not hurting your feelings with not leading you on. It's why I never flirted back. It's like I programmed myself to see you as Hammer's kid daughter and that's what you were. Besides, Hammer would have killed me."

I nod. "I can understand that. But I always thought…" I stop myself.

"No. Tell me," he encourages.

Well, Sky, it's now or never. "I always thought that there was this connection between us. I mean, I knew you never looked at me in a romantic way, but there was something more than friendship. I don't know what I'm saying…" I trail off, afraid to look into his face.

He's silent for a while, and then he grabs my hand. "Sky, look at me."

I do as he asks and see nothing but sincerity and gentleness in his eyes.

"There *was* a connection. You weren't wrong. But you were a kid, and no matter what you felt or I felt, it never would have happened back then, even if you had never left."

And just like that my heart shatters. He's telling me that we're destined to be just friends. I try not to cry.

"I understand," I whisper, trying to hold in the pain that I feel after hearing that.

He looks at me and shakes his head. "No, I don't think you do. What I'm trying to say is it never would've happened then. But you being gone all those years, and coming back as an adult woman…it changes things."

I process what he's saying to me. "So you're saying that it's good that my mother took me away from my only family and stole money meant for me, and that I lived a pitiful existence for five years," I joke.

He laughs. "Well, I'm not saying what happened to you was good. But I'm saying that it changed the course of things. Now we get a fresh start. Now you are an adult. Now I don't have to hold back."

Holy shit, did my childhood crush just tell me that I have a chance?

We're silent as our drinks come.

"So what else have I missed out on? The MC has consumed my life," he admits, a distant look in his eyes. "I've been working my ass off to prove myself, and to slowly work up the rank. How about you? How was country life?"

"Pretty good, but it was the same thing every day, you know? After I moved out of Mom's, she met Neville and they got married and moved in together, and then I kind of fended for myself. Worked at the café to make ends meet, spent a lot of time with my friends." I pause, thinking of Shauna. "I told you about Shauna. She was my best friend, and for a little while there it was always her, me and Max—the Three Musketeers. If I wasn't at work or with them, I was volunteering at the children's hospital. I think I was kind of just buying time while deciding what I should study at college."

"And what did you decide on?"

"Still contemplating," I say, grinning. "Terrible, I know. I'm twenty-one and still have no idea what I want to do with my life."

Saint laughs softly, and reaches over the table to touch the bracelet on my wrist. "Is there anything you're leaning toward? Anything you are passionate about?"

I think about what he is asking me. No one has ever asked me that and I don't think I ever asked myself this either.

"You know I never stopped to ask myself that. I'm not very creative, so being an artist or poet is out. I have issues with authority—let's blame me being raised in an MC for that one—so that's a no to law enforcement," I joke. "But in all seriousness. I think I want to help people. I like helping people. When I was volunteering at the children's hospital, I got a huge sense of satisfaction after my shifts there. Like I was doing something to make another person's day better. Like I was making a difference."

"That doesn't surprise me at all, Sky. You've always been so empathetic. Always wanting to put a smile on someone's face."

"Yeah, but now the question is, how do I turn that into a career?"

"You're still young, and you have time. You'll figure it out."

"You sound so confident," I whisper, eyes on his fingers.

"You're destined for great things," he replies, bringing my gaze back to his. "I've always known it, and I believe in you. That mind is a weapon."

Ducking my head just as the waitress brings us our meal, I thank her then wait for her to leave before saying, "I guess only time will tell."

"And you have all the time in the world," he says, taking a sip of his soda.

"You say the MC has consumed your life. How so? No one ever told me about how the MC was run back then, what you guys did to make ends meet. What exactly do you do for the Knights?"

He studies me for a few seconds before answering. "We have a few different businesses. Security, for one. We do security for high-profile people. We also own and run a bar. We do a few little things on the side, but those are the things I'm not going to mention right now."

My eyes widen. "At least tell me it's not drugs."

He shakes his head, but says nothing else. If they aren't selling drugs, maybe it's weapons, guns or something.

"You're not a pimp, are you? Because that would kind of be a deal breaker."

He shakes his head again, this time with amusement dancing in his eyes.

"Okay, good. What does twenty-six feel like?" I ask, changing the subject to something a little lighter.

"Pretty good," he admits, flashing his teeth in a grin, and placing his glass back down onto the table. "My back's not hurting yet. I think I'll give that another five years or so."

"Nope, it does look like your body is in fine form," I say, leaning forward and lowering my voice. I'm trying my hand at this flirting thing. "Looks like you've spent a lot of time in the gym while I've been gone."

He flexes his arm. "Nice to know my hard work hasn't gone unappreciated."

"Nice to know your ego is still intact," I fire back, amused.

"I don't know what you're talking about," he replies, laughing out loud. "I'm as modest as they come."

"Well, Mr. Modest, are you going to tell me what happened that got you locked up?"

"Got into a fight," is all he says, shrugging. "I lost my cool, hit a guy, and then was arrested. I took a plea deal that gave only a few months in jail. And here I am."

He makes it sound like it's not a big deal at all, when it clearly is.

I let it slide, though, and figure he will open up about it in due time.

It's always been so easy to talk to Saint, and it's good to know that that hasn't changed. We eat, and laugh and joke through the entire meal. It's like I'm getting to know him all over again.

The butter chicken was amazing, but the company was even better.

Chapter Twelve

"Where have you been?" Logan asks as I step inside the house, key still in my hand. "It's ten o'clock—you left hours ago."

"I hung out at the clubhouse then went to eat dinner," I explain, locking the door behind me. "Why, what's wrong?"

"Nothing, I was just worried when you didn't answer your phone."

"Shit, sorry," I murmur, pulling it out of my bag. "It was on silent."

"Hey," Sabrina says as she pokes her head out of their bedroom. "How was your rendezvous with the bikers?"

"Good," I say, smiling. The smile drops as I remember the whole money fiasco. "And also bad. I found out that Hammer left me some money for college, and Mom never gave it to me."

And to think of all the nights I was eating two-minute noodles because I couldn't afford anything else. That hundred thousand would have come in handy. Hell, one thousand dollars would have come in handy.

"Wait, what?" Logan asks, frowning. He follows me into the kitchen, where I put down my bag and grab some water from the sink. "He left you money and she took it? How much are we talking here?" He pauses, and then adds, "And how come the rest of us didn't get any money?"

"It was for me to go to college," I tell him with a shrug. "And because I'm the favorite."

"You totally are, you little shit. With Hammer, anyway. I'm Mom's favorite," he responds, sitting down.

"Is that something to brag about?" I ask, smirking. "And even if you did get any money, Mom probably would have taken that too. Maybe he did leave money for you all. I remember he used to pay for everything for all of us. Anyway, I don't know if I should call her out on it or just let it be. Maybe it's still sitting there in her bank, growing interest. Neville pays for everything for her, so it's not like she has to reach into her own pocket. I knew she was shady, but this is next level. No wonder she never cared when I couldn't decide what to study in college."

"She probably tried to justify it," Logan agrees, shaking his head in shock. "If you ask her about it, that's what she's going to say, that you never enrolled in college so you didn't need the money. Plus if you call her she's going to know that you spoke to Hammer."

"So basically I have to let go of the largest amount of money I'd probably ever see in my life?" I sulk, pouting my lip out. "Damn, I was almost rich there for a second."

"Now you'll actually have to go to college and get a job that pays well," he adds, amusement dancing in his eyes. "Ain't that a bitch?"

I expel a deep sigh. "The search for a desirable career path continues."

Sabrina joins us in the kitchen, her long silk robe trailing behind her. "Man, I'm thirty and I still don't know what I want to do."

"You guys aren't giving me much hope here," I dead-pan. "Don't you like your job at the retirement center, Sabrina?"

She shrugs and moves to stand next to Logan. "Pays the bills. I don't love it, though. I always wanted to get a job in fashion, design my own clothes or something."

"Why don't you?" I ask. "If I knew what I wanted, I'd be going after it."

"I don't know, I guess I didn't think it was something that was realistic," she admits, sounding saddened by that fact. "Only a few people would be making money off those type of jobs. Working as a nurse's aide is steady pay, and there's lots of work. Fashion is a gamble. But maybe I should look into it. I'm in a more stable place now, or I could even take it on as a hobby."

"You should," I encourage.

A gamble.

Why do I feel like anything worth pursuing is usually a gamble?

"What are you doing here?" I ask Saint, smiling up at him. He looks like a damn snack, dressed in black from head to toe, his bound hair off his face.

"Wanted to check out your new workplace," he replies, glancing around the bar before bringing his eyes back to me. "And I wanted to ask you out on a date."

My eyes widen. "A date?"

I can't stop the smile spreading on my face. I had hoped after getting dinner the other night that he was into me, but I didn't really know for sure. When we got back to the clubhouse to get my car he just gave me a hug and said he'd see me around.

He nods, eyes pinning me in my place. "Things are different now, Sky. Do you understand what I'm saying?"

Talk about putting me on the spot. "So the Indian food wasn't a date?"

"More like a pre-date catch-up," he replies, shrugging. "So are we on the same page?"

"Yes," I say, swallowing hard. "I mean, I think so."

"You think or you know?" he asks, lip twitching.

"You want me," I state, boldly so.

And he's letting me know it, clear as day.

He nods and flashes me that smile of his, the one that makes me feel weak in the knees. "How about tomorrow night? I thought maybe I could take you for a ride on my bike."

I know the men are weird about who they let on their bikes, and once they're taken they want only their old ladies on the back of theirs.

"That sounds nice," I reply, happiness filling me. "Do you want something to drink while you're here?"

"Sure, I'll have a whiskey. Neat, please," he says, taking some money out of his wallet while I make the drink. He gives me a hundred dollar bill, then shakes his head when I try to give him the change, so I put it all in the tip jar.

"You're ridiculous, you know that?" I tell him as I slide him his drink.

He simply grins. "Thank you."

"You're welcome. Are you going to stick around?"

"Yeah, for a bit anyway," he says. "I've never been here before."

And I bet he wants to suss the place out, probably see what type of crowd we get. It's pretty much a standard bar, though, with a dance floor thrown in. "It's a pretty easygoing place, Saint. I'm fine. It starts to get busier in about an hour."

"Let me do my thing, and I'll let you do yours," he murmurs, lip twitching, making my eyes narrow.

"You going to start trying to boss me around before we've even gone on our first date?" I ask, arching my brow with my hands on my hips. "I didn't take any of your shit before I was even legal—don't think I'm going to take it now."

He throws back his head and laughs.

And it's glorious.

"I don't know what's so funny," I grumble, grabbing a cloth and wiping down the counter so my boss doesn't see me doing nothing. "I might not have had many boyfriends, but I know what I'm not going to put up with."

"Boyfriend, hey?" he teases, leaning forward over the counter. "I think you're moving a little too fast for me, Sky."

I throw the cloth at him and storm to the other side of the bar, shaking my head in amusement and embarrassment. He's such a shithead.

Saint follows me, glass of whiskey still in his hand, and glances out over the dance floor, where there's only a couple of people enjoying the music.

"You still like singing?" He turns back to me to ask, finishing the rest of his drink and placing the glass down.

"You remember that?" I ask, eyes widening in surprise. "Yeah, I still like singing. Just not in front of anyone. I'm more of a bathroom singer."

"Yeah, you used to sing while doing your homework at the table in the clubhouse," he reminisces, leaning over the table and touching my cheek. "You were in school while I was prospecting."

"It was a big age gap at the time," I admit, shrugging. "But it doesn't feel that way now. Does it to you?"

"It doesn't feel that way now, no," he agrees, pushing an errant hair back behind my ear.

Some customers appear, and I take a step away from him, pull myself together and go do my job, while Saint faces the crowd. I don't actually mind him being here, but I realize it's going to be a problem when the place starts to fill up and the women start to approach him.

The first one—who is very beautiful, might I add—strolls up to him confidently and speaks to him with her hand on his arm. He removes it, which I appreciate, and shakes his head at her, refusing whatever she had on offer.

Scowling, I make two espresso martinis, trying not to glance back over at him. I know he's here because he's being protective, but apart from the eye candy, he's not helping, and I'm perfectly safe. I also seem to be paying more attention to what he is doing than the customers lining up for drinks. The man is a distraction.

The next time I look there's two new women trying to speak to him.

"Do you want to have a break, Skylar?" Camilla, the bar manager, asks me.

"Yes, please," I tell her, not moving my eyes from Saint.

"Is that your man?" she asks me, whistling under her breath. "He's fine."

"Not yet, but he will be," I reply, walking around the bar and straight to him. His eyes widen as he sees me, but it doesn't stop me from my mission. I step through the women, right in front of him, get up on my tiptoes and kiss him.

I wanted this kiss long before I was ever going to get it, so different from the innocent kiss Saint gave me all those years ago before I was ripped out of his arms.

And fuck.

His soft lips respond immediately as he takes control, gently gripping the back of my neck and pulling me closer to him. I have goose bumps on my skin, and my heart is racing out of my chest as he kisses me like I've never been kissed before, sensually yet hungrily. The kiss gets a little too hot for public, his tongue teasing me and our bodies pressed up and close as they can get with our clothes on.

It's me who pulls away. "Wow," I whisper, licking my lips and staring up at him.

He swipes his thumb along my lower lip. "You're moving too fast for me, Sky," he teases again, wrapping an arm around me and kissing the top of my head. "What was that for?"

I decide to stay silent, because anything I say right now isn't going to make me look good. Instead, I glance at the two women, who are still standing on either side of him, watching us. Apparently they just can't take a hint.

Saint leans down and whispers into my ear. "And by the way, these are my cousins."

His cousins?

Shit.

"This is Skylar," he says to the two of them. "Skylar, this is Jamila and Daisy. They're my mom's brother's daughters."

Fucking hell. Clearing my throat, I manage to get out

a "Nice to meet you both." I can feel my face heating, embarrassment creeping in.

"This is all your fault," I whisper-yell at Saint.

"What is my fault?" he asks, amusement written all over him.

"You were standing here distracting me all night," I say, not wanting to mention how worked up seeing all the women trying to hit on him got me, even though he must know that's the reason I stormed over here in the first place.

As I start to calm down, I realize how stupid I must look right now, and what a mistake I've made.

He's not even mine—he just asked me on a date, and I'm already marking my damn territory. I might as well have peed on him right here in front of everyone, including the new people I work with.

Fucking hell, Skylar.

Chapter Thirteen

I can sense his amusement while I make small talk with his cousins, who are gracious enough not to hold my behavior against me. They don't seem too surprised by what I did, seeing as they have apparently heard about me from Saint before and are happy finally to have met me.

"I better get back to work," I tell them both. "It was nice meeting you."

And sorry about being a dickhead.

"I'm going to head off too," Saint says, lowering to kiss my forehead. Butterflies fill my stomach. I don't know how it's so natural for us to be affectionate after everything we've been through. I had a crush on him and he was too old for me, but now we are on an even playing field, which is hard to wrap my mind around. "Call me if you need anything, and let me know if you need a ride home. Anything, all right?"

"I'll be fine. And don't even think about sending Dee or someone else to come here and keep an eye on me," I tell him, shaking my head at the thought.

"Damn, when Dee shows up here tell him to go home," he jokes, saying goodbye to his cousins and walking me back around the bar. "Do you want me to pick you up after work?"

"No," I tell him, rolling my eyes. "My car is here. I'll be fine."

"Okay," he grumbles, leaning me back against the counter and kissing me properly. Melting into him, I suddenly wish I wasn't at work, although who knows if I'm even going to have my job after my display tonight.

I'm breathless when he lifts his head, blue eyes filled with heat. "I better go."

"I think you should," I whisper, clearing my throat.

He flashes me a wide smile, then leaves.

Dusting off my work shirt, I turn back to see Camilla watching us with wide eyes. *That was hot*, she mouths, fanning herself.

Cheeks heating, I step back behind the bar, in professional mode once more.

Saint is a bad, bad influence on me.

The next morning, staring at the word *Mom* on my phone, I let it go to voicemail. She's the last person I want to talk to right now.

It rings again, this time from Neville's phone, but I ignore that too. I'm not that stupid.

There's a knock on my bedroom door. "Come in!"

Logan peeps his head in before stepping inside. "What you doing?"

"Nothing much," I admit, glancing down at my phone next to me on the bed. "Wondering what Mom wants."

"Yeah, she tried to call me too," he says, sitting down in the cane chair opposite my bed. "So what's been going on?"

"You mean besides the whole Saint thing?"

"You always liked him," he grumbles. "What's going to happen with the two of you?"

My mind flashes back to last night, when we had our first kiss—and better yet, it was me who kissed him and not the other way around. "I don't know," I reply, sitting up and studying him. "It's too early to tell. Why? You don't approve of him?"

"I didn't say that. I'm just wondering," he muses, keeping his expression blank. "Is that what you want to do with your life? Be a Knights old lady? I know that you grew up with the club, but a lot of what goes down there was shielded from you."

"I know you think I was shielded from most things, but I'm not stupid," I tell him, frowning. "I do have feelings for Saint, though, and if it doesn't work out with him, I wouldn't try to find another Knights member. I mean, my end goal is not to be somebody's old lady, but I can't help who I feel a connection with. Saint has always been one of my favorite people. It's not about the club, it's about him."

"I didn't mean that you just wanted to be an old lady to anyone, Sky. I just wanted to ask if this is how you want your life to be. Being with Saint comes with a lot of shit, and I just don't want you to be blinded by a teenage crush and distracted by all that hair and muscle. You do know what kind of shit they must be involved in, right? That much money doesn't come from a nine-to-five."

I laugh out loud at his description of him. "Thank you for the concern, Logan. I do know what you mean and are worried about. But with Saint, it's not really a choice, you know? I mean, I don't know if things will work out or if we will end up together, but I do know that if I don't try then I'm always going to wonder what if. So if this whole thing ends up being one huge mistake, I'm going to have to live with that and take that chance."

And because I haven't met any other man who so much as holds my attention.

It's always been Saint.

Maybe Logan is right and I *am* blinded by some crush that started years ago, but it still doesn't change how I feel and what I want.

"When's the last time you saw Saint?" I ask Logan. "With all his hair and muscle."

He rolls his eyes. "It's been a while. I stopped coming by the clubhouse, what, six months before you left for the country? So it would have been then."

"Years, then."

"Yep. Almost same as you. Okay," he says, nodding. "As long as you know what you're getting yourself into. I just don't want to see you get hurt. I feel like Mom got even crazier after Hammer ended things with her. You have to be strong to deal with those men."

"And you don't think I am?" I ask him.

"No, it's not that. I just don't see why you have to be," he admits, tapping his fingers on the arm of the chair. "Why do you need to become tougher, and more resilient, when with an average man you wouldn't have to? You wouldn't need to get used to him being around women and all the hangers-on, you wouldn't need to worry about where he is every night and if he's safe, or if he's gotten himself locked up again. You wouldn't need to worry about any of that. The road you're choosing is yours to decide, but you're choosing the harder path."

He smiles to soften the blow, and leaves my bedroom.

But his words linger long after his exit.

Later that night, I'm climbing on the back of Saint's motorcycle in tight ripped jeans, a Freddie Mercury

T-shirt, black block heels and Saint's leather jacket. He hasn't told me exactly where we are going, other than to go for a ride and get something to eat, so I thought I'd wear something that would work no matter where the night takes us.

It's been so long since I've been on the back of a bike, and that was only on Hammer's or Temper's, so this is a whole different ball game. After Logan's words this morning, I must admit I'm a bit more on guard. But I need to make my own choices and decisions. And I need to try.

"You ready?" Saint asks, placing his hands on mine when I wrap my fingers around him.

"Yep!" I call back to him. The helmet feels a little more claustrophobic than I remember, but as soon as he takes off and the wind is hitting me, it's not so bad.

I take in everything—the smells, the sights, the sounds, the wind on my face and in my hair, and the sense of freedom that comes from the ride—just enjoying this little moment, after having missed this elated feeling for so long. As we breeze through traffic, I notice a lot of people looking at us, even without Saint wearing his Knights cut, and wonder what they are thinking.

When Saint slows down and pulls over onto the side of the road, I have no idea what he's doing until I see what's happening on the other side. Two cars have collided, and it's the biggest crash I've seen with my own eyes. One of the cars doesn't look too bad, but the other one is completely smashed, the windshield and windows all broken and the whole front bumper crushed.

"Shit," I whisper, removing my helmet and jumping off the bike after Saint stops on the side of the road. "That doesn't look good."

"Call the ambulance," Saint tells me, heading over to the car wreck just as more people stop to help, examining the car for any other survivors.

I pull my phone out of Saint's jacket pocket and dial 9-1-1, watching as Saint opens one of the car doors and speaks to the person inside. After telling the lady on the line about what happened and where we are, I hang up and follow Saint, who has a man in front of him lying on the ground.

"How bad is my head?" I hear the man asking Saint, touching the blood on his forehead. "My chest hurts too. Is everyone else okay? Oh my God, I hope they're okay."

"Keep this on there," Saint tells the man, ripping cloth off his flannelette jacket and using it to stop the bleeding. The man holds the blue material against his wound, which is soon drenched with blood.

"Fuck," I hear Saint mutter, then quickly moves to help the next person, who is screaming out with a leg injury.

Just as Saint moves away, the man loses consciousness. When I check on him, I notice that he's not breathing.

Fuck.

Following the first aid training I recently did at my old job at the café, something I thought was a waste at the time, I clear his airways and proceed to give him CPR. Pumping down on his chest, I count each push in my head then lower my mouth to his to breathe into it.

When I pull back and he starts to breathe again, I close my eyes and look up at the night sky in relief.

The ambulance pulls up shortly, and Saint and I watch as they take away the four people involved in the accident, all with varying injuries.

"You were amazing," he says to me, pulling me closer. "You saved that man's life, and you didn't panic. I'm so proud of you, Sky."

"You helped all of them," I say in return. "And you were the first to stop and help. Lots of people didn't even bother."

"Some did, though," he mutters, absently touching my waist.

As I pull back from him, I notice something. "You have blood on you. Do you want to go and clean up before we do anything else?" I'm not really in the mood to go and sit at a fancy restaurant after everything that has just happened anyway. I feel like having a steaming hot shower and curling up in bed with soup or something.

"Yeah, maybe we should move date night to another night," he says, exactly what I was thinking. "Come on, let's go back to the clubhouse."

We get on the bike and ride back the way that we came.

A lot slower, this time.

Chapter Fourteen

After my long, hot shower, I leave the bathroom in a towel, another one wrapped around my hair. I pretend I don't notice him watching me. "Shower is free."

"Thanks," he says, standing up from the bed, bloody T-shirt gone and nothing but smooth skin and muscles left in its place. "I ordered us some food in."

"Sounds perfect," I reply, eyes lingering on the indentation under his pecs, and down farther to the vee right underneath the top of his jeans.

"Don't look at me like that, Sky," he rumbles, walking past me and into the bathroom. I turn to catch an eye of his muscular back before the door shuts. I never even knew backs could be sexy, but boy, they can.

My body starts to overheat, and I feel a little clammy. After sliding the towel off my body and onto the bed, I change into the T-shirt he left for me to wear as I hear the shower turn back on.

We haven't really had a talk about my lack of experience in the bedroom, and I know it's something that is very different about us. He's older and has slept with plenty of women, while all I've done is kiss and had a few hands go wandering. While I'm not embarrassed about the fact that I'm still a virgin, I know it's just a reminder of how young I am. Still, if he wants me he's going to have to deal with whatever I come with, and me the same with him.

I'm sitting on the bed going through my phone when Saint walks out in his towel, and I can't help but stare at him. I may be drooling and I really don't care. He shakes his head at me, but the little smile on his mouth lets me know he likes the way I look at him.

"What?" I ask, not ashamed in the least. "You are sexy." Feeling bold, I add, "Can I touch you?"

I know it may sound like I'm inviting him to bed, but I genuinely just want to touch him. I've imagined touching him for years and here he is, with us in this weird limbo place. I figure it's worth the ask.

He stays still, so I move toward him and reach out to touch his shoulders and the soft skin there, then his hard biceps, then down his chest and ripped abs. He is all muscle, and I could touch him all day, the concept so foreign to me.

"Any farther and you're gonna be in trouble, Sky," he says in a husky tone, eyes locked on mine.

Now would probably be the right time to tell him.

"I'm a virgin," I blurt out, anticipating his reaction. "So you're going to have to take it slow with me."

Blue eyes widen, and his fingers reach out to touch my face. "You're the most beautiful woman I've ever laid my eyes on, and you've managed to get to your twenties a virgin? You're a fucking unicorn, is what you are." He rests his forehead against mine. "You control the pace, Sky. I want you, but I'm not going to rush you. We can go as slow as you want to."

He kisses me then, a sweet, gentle kiss. The kiss of a man who is going to enjoy the journey instead of rushing to the end. The thing is, I'm more ready than I let on. I haven't stayed a virgin because I wasn't ready for sex; I stayed one because no one was Saint, and now that he's here and he's said exactly what I want to hear, I don't think I'm going to last long without wanting him to be the first man inside me.

"You'll wait for me," I ask, smiling against his lips.

"You're worth it," he replies. "You know you were the only one who ever understood me, even back when we were just nothing but friends and I was a prospect. You always said just what I needed to hear."

"You can be pretty closed off," I say gently, placing my palm on his chest. "You know you can trust me, right? You don't need to have your walls up around me."

"I know," he whispers.

"What did Hammer say about us?"

"That if I hurt you he will skin me alive," he admits, cringing. "But he knows that we've always gravitated toward each other. I don't think anyone is surprised, to be honest. If anything I think I'm more surprised than anyone else."

His hand roams down the back of the T-shirt I'm wearing until it rests on my ass. "Are you wearing any panties?"

I shake my head.

He makes a deep sound in the back of his throat. "You're not going to make this easy on me, are you?"

"I feel like you've had enough easy," I tease, stepping back and winking at him. "Time for a bit of a challenge for once."

"You're making a lot of assumptions here, Sky," he murmurs, gaze on my thighs.

"And are they true or false?" I ask.

He laughs out loud. "True, but still, you don't need to call me out on it."

Picking me up, he throws me back on the bed, his T-shirt going up in the air and flashing him before I can pin it down, making me squeal.

Saint simply laughs, our eyes cutting to the door as someone knocks.

"Stop giggling away in there!" Hammer shouts out. "The food is here!"

We laugh harder.

Saint makes me wear a bra and jeans under his T-shirt before he lets me leave the room. When I enter the kitchen and see everyone, I can understand why. Temper arches his brow when he sees me, glancing between Saint, me and Hammer before shaking his head in an "I don't even want to know" manner.

"Hello, Temper," I say cheerfully, sitting down and glancing around the table. "Dee," I say in a less excited tone. "How are we all?"

Dee just laughs and Temper throws a chip at me.

"Not quite the date night I had in mind," I say to Saint, who grins and kisses my cheek. "I'll make it up to you later this week. I didn't plan on getting covered in blood before we could even have dinner."

"What happened?" Temper asks, and Saint recaps our night for him.

"Sky was amazing—she gave one of the men CPR and literally saved his life. She was solid."

"I was terrified, but I knew panicking wasn't going to help anyone," I admit. "And the feeling of saving someone was exhilarating. Like I would have done anything to save that man. I don't know how to explain it."

I glance around the table to see all the men staring at me. "What?" I ask.

"Your eyes just lit up," Hammer says, sitting back in his chair. "Maybe you're meant to be a doctor or nurse, or a paramedic. I know you were up in the air about what you want to do, but I think this might be your calling."

"Yeah, and we could always use a doctor around here," Temper adds, smirking. "Someone is always getting hurt, or shot, and no one wants to go and see a doctor and have to explain that shit."

The men all make sounds of agreement.

"Don't try and make this about you," I tease, sitting back and contemplating Hammer's words. He might be right.

Saint agrees. "You have it in you, if that's what you want to do, Sky. Honestly, you surprised me tonight. Most people freak out and panic in situations like that."

Interesting. Could I see myself in the medical field? The excitement that fills me at the thought says yes. It's about time I did something with my life—working in hospitality isn't my calling and I've always known that.

"I'll have to look into it," I say, smiling wide.

"And don't worry about money," Saint says to me quietly. "I'll cover anything you need."

I open my mouth to object, but Hammer interrupts me. "Money isn't an issue, Skylar. Find out what you want to do and enroll in it. And you can even quit the job at the seedy bar too."

"Yeah, or I'll be in there more to check on you, and you know how that went the other night," Saint adds, chuckling to himself.

"What did we miss?" Renny asks, looking between us.

I sit there red-faced as Saint tells them the story about

his cousins and me being jealous, thinking that they were random women trying to hit on him.

"Very funny, guys. Just wait until the tables are turned—I bet it won't be funny then," I tell them all, huffing.

"It will still be funny, actually," Temper adds, shoving a chip dipped in salsa in his mouth. "Watching Saint beat the shit out of someone and get arrested is pretty amusing."

"What?" I ask, confused.

"How do you think he got arrested the first time?" Dee adds, shrugging. "He lost his temper."

That's right. Saint told me this at dinner, although apparently it was seriously downplayed. "Temper, maybe you and Saint need to swap road names," I mutter.

This is what Logan meant. This is everyday life for them, and I knew Saint went to prison, obviously, but hearing them play it off like that and turn it into a joke is hard to listen to.

And the question is, will it happen a second time?

Chapter Fifteen

"Who did you attack that got you locked up, Saint?" I ask the next morning. We had spent the rest of the night watching a movie and then fell asleep cuddling. And now that the sun is up, I realize we have to have this discussion. I can't not ask.

He sighs deeply and rolls over to face me. "I got drunk and was out at a club, and I got into a fight. They arrested me. I told you this. I accepted the plea deal, did my time and now I'm out."

That doesn't answer my question.

"Does stuff like that happen often?" I press.

"No," he replies quickly. "Sometimes other shit happens, though. I'm not a saint, Sky." His lip twitches when he realizes what he just said. "I mean, I'm a biker, and you know sometimes we get into trouble, and it's not always my trouble. I protect and defend all of my brothers, just as they do with me. You know all of this."

"I do, and I guess I just want to know exactly what I'm getting myself into," I admit. "I haven't been here, and when I was, you guys never let me see the bad. I don't know if you getting into a fight is a common occurrence or not, so I'm just asking so I know what to expect."

"Are you thinking you might not be able to handle

this before anything has even happened?" he asks me quietly, tucking my hair back behind my ear. "I've only been arrested one time. It's not an everyday thing, and I'm not going out there looking for fights. I am able to control myself, but yes, that time I was drunk and lost my shit, and I have paid for that. I have no desire to go back to prison for anything. I didn't have anything to lose before, and now I do, okay?"

"Okay," I breathe, considering his words. "And no, it's not that I'm not going to be able to handle whatever happens, I just want you to be honest with me, that's all. I don't like hearing information from the other people; I should hear it from you. I might not be a professional at relationships, but I know that communication is key."

He looks away from me, then sits up and stares ahead. "Yeah, you're right. Communication. Loyalty. Honestly." He turns back to me. "I want all of this with you, all right? I'm not fucking around here. You mean something to me. You always have. You're not just another woman."

"Good, we're on the same page then," I reply, pulling him back down and onto me. "Tell me something."

"Like what?"

"Anything," I whisper.

"Okay." He thinks, laying his head on my chest without putting all of his weight on me. "I had a dream last night, and it was weird. We had a son together."

"That's an interesting dream to have," I whisper, smiling to myself.

Saint goes quiet, and I run my fingers through his hair.

As much as Logan's words had truth to them, I know in my heart he is wrong.

And I'm going to prove it.

* * *

I find a two-year degree program in paramedic training. I looked into nursing and even becoming a doctor, but that would be something I need to dedicate my whole life to, and I'd have to be willing to move to wherever I'm needed. I think working in paramedics I'd enjoy being on the go and the adrenaline of being the first at different scenes instead of being stuck in a hospital. Something new every day.

I'm glad Hammer said money isn't an issue, because the paramedic program is almost ten thousand dollars in fees. Although compared to going to med school, that's basically nothing.

"So you're serious about this?" Logan asks as we sit and have a coffee in front of the TV. "I think it's pretty cool."

"Yeah, I think so. I'm really excited about it, actually," I tell him, blowing on the hot liquid. "I feel like maybe it is my calling. Nothing else has got me motivated like this. Normally I'd just check out the courses, do the research but then do nothing about it."

"Are you going to enroll?"

"Yeah, I'm going to go in this week. There's a month before the next program starts, so I have time to sort everything out. Hammer and Saint want me to quit the bar, but I don't think I'm going to. I need my own money; I don't want to rely on them for everything."

"Probably smart," Logan agrees. "I spoke to Mom. The entire time she was asking about you and whether you tried to see Hammer."

"What did you say?" I ask, rolling my eyes at how nosy she is.

"I told her I had no idea, that you got a job and work a lot," he says, shrugging. "If I tell her about Hammer and Saint, she will probably drive straight here just to stir shit up."

"What, and bring Neville? Hammer will chew him up and spit him out. And he's a nice guy—he doesn't deserve to be dragged into Mom's shit," I admit, feeling bad for him.

"She could come here without him. She'd just say she wants to see you," he replies, pausing and then adding, "But yeah, he'd definitely try to tag along. He's a bit of a stage-five clinger."

"Or he's just smarter than we give him credit for and doesn't trust leaving Mom alone," I mutter, taking a sip from the Harry Potter mug, then putting it down on the coffee table in front of me. "I should have just answered the phone because now she's going to know something is up. I shouldn't have to play these games with her, though. It's bullshit."

"She's never just going to accept that you are back in the MC life and she's not," Logan concludes, running a hand through his hair. "She hated that she got dumped and lost everything, all her power. No more connections, money, nothing. She was suddenly just a normal woman with a heap of kids and no man again."

"She needs to let it go," I grumble, picking up my phone and smiling when I see there is a text message from Saint.

I miss you. What are you doing tonight?

Working, I type back, then add, And no, that wasn't an invitation for you to join me.

What a shame, I wouldn't mind one of those kisses again, he instantly replies, making me laugh out loud.

"You have it bad," Logan says, shaking his head at me. Sabrina comes into the room and cuddles up next to him.

"So when am I going to meet this man of yours?" she asks me, kind brown eyes curious.

"I don't know," I tell her. "Next time he picks me up I can bring him in and introduce you."

"Sounds good," she replies, perking up. "I've heard about the Knights, but I've never met any of them. I know Logan speaks to their Hammer on the phone, but that's all the fun we get around here."

"Probably for the best," I mutter, and Logan makes a sound of agreement. "Logan, remember that birthday party Mom threw for you in the clubhouse?"

"The one I never turned up to?" he asks in a dry tone, nodding. "Yeah, I remember. I told her I didn't want a party, especially not there, I just wanted a dinner with the family, but she went and did the party anyway. Not really my scene, so I said fuck it and decided not to show. I spent the night with Sabrina instead." He turns to her and says, "Remember? You took me out for the quiet dinner I originally wanted."

"Yeah, and your phone kept going off with everyone asking you where the hell you were," she says, amusement in her eyes. "That was such a long time ago. I think we'd pretty much just met and weren't even exclusive then."

"Wow, I thought the whole nonexclusive thing was just with modern dating," I muse, laughing when Logan sends a glare in my direction.

"I'm not that old, thank you," he replies, softening as he looks back to Sabrina. "But yeah, we were just casual when we met. I wasn't really looking for a relationship. I had so much family drama going on and wasn't in the best place, but I couldn't let her pass me by. She's a once-in-a-lifetime type of woman, so I had to man up."

"That's a bit cute," I whisper, chin resting on my palm and watching the two of them. "And you guys have lasted for so long. If I need relationship advice, I'm coming to the both of you." I pause, and then amend, "Well, maybe just you, Sabrina. I don't think Logan wants to know too much information."

Sabrina laughs, shoulders shaking. "I'm always here if you need advice or someone to vent to. It's actually nice having another girl around. I'm an only child, and before you moved in it was just your brothers randomly dropping in with alcohol and eating all of our food."

"I'm still eating all your food," I point out, grinning. "Speaking of, I want to take you both out for dinner to say thank you for letting me stay here, and for being the family I always wanted, pretty much."

"You don't have to—"

"I want to." And now that I've made a little money from working, and with tips, I can afford to.

"Don't worry about us, Sky. You should be saving your money," says Logan, always the wise one.

"Just let me say thank you," I say. "I know it's not much, but let me do this, at least. I'm very grateful to you both for making my move here such an easy, amazing one."

"Okay," he says, grinning. "When do you want to do this? Tomorrow night? We can go to McDonalds."

Rolling my eyes, I say, "I was going for something a little fancier. You two can choose."

I stand up and kiss Logan on the cheek, then head up to my room.

I have a program to enroll in.

Chapter Sixteen

The next night after dinner with Logan and Sabrina at a Sri Lankan restaurant, Saint texts and asks me if I can come to the clubhouse to spend the night.

I bring some takeaway food with me for him and Hammer, and step into the clubhouse. There's loud music playing, so the men must be drinking or maybe having people over, who knows. I didn't see Hammer's bike out the front, so he may not be here tonight.

More food for me.

I put the food in the kitchen, and then find Saint sitting out back with a beer in his hand, laughing with Renny about something or another, but he stands with a wide smile when he sees me.

"Hello, beautiful," he murmurs, strolling over to me and lifting me up in his arms. He gives me a quick kiss, and then pulls me down onto his lap. I notice that there are other members here tonight, new faces, and a few women around the place. All eyes are on me.

"How was dinner?" he asks.

"Good. I brought you some food," I reply, turning on his lap to face him.

"You spoil me," he says with a grin. "Do you want something to drink? Beer? Juice? Soda? I stocked the fridge and cupboard for you. I think I might have gone overboard."

"I'm fine, but thank you," I say, kissing him again quickly.

"Hey, Sky," Renny calls out.

I move my face around Saint, who was blocking him with his body. "Renegade. How are you?"

"I'm good. Even better now that we're eating like kings since you came back," he teases, lifting a beer up in cheers. "Although I'm going to have to do extra hours in the gym," he grumbles, raising his white T-shirt, showing off a very toned six-pack of abs. I don't think he has to worry about that just yet.

"Happy to be of service," I tell him, grinning, then glance back up at Saint. "What kind of stuff did you buy?"

"I didn't know what cereal you liked, so I got a variety. Bacon, eggs, stuff to make pancakes, juice. Snacks. Everything," he says with a shrug. "I remember you used to like strawberry-frosted cupcakes, so I got some of those too. And mangoes."

"You are so fucking cute," I say, warmth filling me. "Mangoes are still my favorite, and I still love those cupcakes."

The fact that he remembers all these things means so much to me. We're both getting to know each other again, but a lot of me is still the same. He knows who I was, and now he's getting to know who I am, and vice versa.

"Good," he murmurs, scanning my face. "Thanks for coming to spend the night with me. I missed you today."

"I missed you too," I say. I'm about to open my mouth

and tell him about how I enrolled in the paramedic course when the door opens and Hammer walks outside.

With none other than my mother.

"What is she doing here?" Saint asks, standing up and putting me next to him, protecting me.

"I asked myself the same thing," Hammer growls, jaw tight and face redder than I've seen it. He must have just arrived at the clubhouse. "I found her standing out the front and demanding to see Skylar, because otherwise she's going to call the cops and tell them that we're keeping her against her will."

"I'm fine, Mom," I tell her, frowning. "And Logan told you I was fine. You didn't have to come all this way."

We all know this isn't about me—this is about her. She never wanted me to reconnect to the MC, because it meant leaving her behind in a different world. I think she sees this as her territory, her old family, and without her I'm not allowed to be in it.

"My own daughter, a traitor," she muses, shaking her head. "I should have known. I never trusted you, you know. From the day you were born, I wished you'd been another boy."

Anger fills me. "How am I a traitor? You are the one who brought Hammer into my life, to be my father figure and to raise me. Just because he broke up with you doesn't mean he broke up with me, even though that's what you wanted!"

"Don't let them fill your head with their lies, Skylar. I am your mother!" she shouts back, pointing at me.

"Why are you here?" I ask, scowling. "No one wants you here, Mom."

She glances around the outdoor area, taking in all

the faces and people, before bringing her gaze back to me. "Leave with me right now or you are dead to me, Skylar. If you don't walk out of these doors, as far as I'm concerned, I have no daughter." She lifts her chin and narrows her eyes. "And you will have no mother."

"Has she ever had a mother?" Hammer asks her, tone as violent as I've ever heard it. "I tell you what, the truth about what happened needs to fucking come out. I wanted to protect Sky from it, but maybe it's better that she knows the truth. So she can understand what happened back then when you took her away from us."

I step closer, needing to hear this. "I want to know the truth."

"Don't listen to a word he says," Mom spits out, but I don't miss the flash of fear in her eyes.

What has she done?

Hammer tells everyone to clear out, except me, Saint, him and Mom. I'm starting to feel really fucking nervous right now, and scared. As Hammer prepares to tell me the truth, hesitating and rubbing the back of his neck, I realize words can't be taken back, and I feel like shit is going to change.

He moves closer to me while my mother just stands there, knowing that she invited this. "Five years ago, we were having a lot of trouble with a rival MC, the Destined Killers," he starts, looking me in the eye. "We'd always coexisted peacefully, but something happened that had them coming after us. Targeting us. Fights broke out, property destroyed, all of that bullshit, until eventually shit went too far. After being hit on the head, one of their members died at our hands. It was an accident. No one meant for anyone to die."

Swallowing hard, I don't know what to say, so I say

nothing. One of the Knights killed someone? Hammer doesn't say who it is, and I don't ask. I'm curious to know who, though. Saint's hands squeeze into fists, as if the memory frustrates him.

"Their president, Killer, was out for blood over it, and said he wasn't going to stop until I was dead," Hammer recaps. "This man is known for liking younger girls, younger than is legal, if you know what I mean. And your mother here suggested, to save my ass…" He trails off, struggling to say the next words. "That we offer you up to him instead."

My jaw drops open. "Offer me up as in…"

As in give me to a fucking adult man?

I eye the woman who gave birth to me, so much pain and anger and betrayal filling me. "You'd give me up to be raped to save your boyfriend? Is that how much I mean to you?"

"No, it's how much he—" she looks to Hammer "—meant to me. He was going to be killed. I was desperate and—"

"You're a monster. I was sixteen years old!" I scream, cutting her off. Saint's arms come around me and I melt into him. I thought I was safe with my own mother, but I was wrong. I was never safe, and she never loved or cared about me. "So that's why you broke up?"

Hammer nods. "That's when I realized just how fucking evil she is, even by my standards. I had fucked up, though, because she knew a lot of shit about the club, and after I dumped her, I told her I wanted to keep you here with me, that she didn't deserve to have you as a daughter. She said if we tried to contact you in any way, she was going to the cops with the information she had on the club. And she knew about every deal we were a part of, our contacts, everything." He looks at me, sadness in his eyes. "I couldn't risk the club."

"So you knew that she didn't give a fuck about me, would have given me to your enemy, but you sent me off with her anyway just so the club didn't get into any shit?" I recap, my chest tightening.

I know the MC is everything to him, but I was just a girl. A girl he claimed to love like his own flesh and blood, and I can't help but feel betrayed over this. They knew, even more than me, what she was like and what she was capable of, but they allowed themselves to be blackmailed by her. They, in all their power, didn't come up with a way to save me from her.

"It's complicated, Skylar," he says, voice soft and broken. "The whole MC could have ended up in prison, and because I'm not your biological father, I wouldn't have been able to keep you without her agreement anyway. She's a spiteful bitch, so she would have fought just so I couldn't have you. She'd have taken me to court, and I wouldn't have a leg to stand on. They'd take one look at who I am and laugh in my face. There was nothing I could do."

Something. He could have done something. Or tried something.

Anything.

No one thought of me.

No one tried to save me.

Yes, Hammer wanted me to stay here, but in the end, he chose the club over me, and I guess this is the point Logan was trying to get across.

The club will always be first.

"Saint rode down to the country to try to see you without us knowing, did you know that?" Hammer asks me.

"You men are all the same!" Mom yells, starting to

pace. "Skylar is my daughter—you aren't her father, Hammer, no matter how much you want to be. She is *mine*."

I push down my anguish at Hammer's admission to face my mother. "What about the money, Mom?" I ask, moving closer to face her. "What did you do with my money?"

"I was owed that money," she sneers, pausing to look at Hammer. "For all the bullshit I did for you, and for this club. I walked away with nothing. I know how much you had in your bank, Hammer. You didn't leave me a cent!"

"I left that money for Skylar's future," he says to her, remaining calm somehow. "Not for you. I knew she wasn't going to see all of it, because you're a selfish bitch, but I thought you'd give her something. Something! I wish I never gave you that account, and I only did it because it was before that bullshit, before I saw you for who you truly are."

She lunges at Hammer, but I move quickly, stepping in front of him. "Don't you dare touch him!" I yell, hands shaking.

She stops, but I know she wants to hit me. She looks me right in the eye, and I don't miss the hate there. Maybe it's always been there, but I'm noticing it only now.

"Touch her and see what happens," Saint says from behind me, his tone as lethal as I've ever heard it. The threat is clear. If she puts her hands on me, she's going to regret it.

"That money was mine," she maintains. "I clothed you and fed you, and you have never had anything to complain about, so don't act all woe is me, Sky. It doesn't suit you."

"So you took my college fund as child support? Or so you keep saying," I fire back, jaw tight. "Have some dignity. You are pathetic—I'll never be like you."

I look back at Saint, who looks as sad as I feel right now. "You came and saw me?"

He nods. "I just had to see you with my own eyes and make sure you were okay. You were at school and with a girl, and the two of you were laughing."

"Shauna," I whisper. I would have been laughing with Shauna, my best friend who passed away.

"I left after that. I wanted to speak to you, but I know I would have jeopardized everyone, and Hammer would have fucking killed me," he admits. "We just needed a little time to bury some shit; we weren't going to let Georgia hold something over us."

"So she doesn't have anything on you now?" I ask.

Hammer shakes his head, glancing over at her with a smug look. "Nope. Nothing. It took us a while, but we handled what we needed to and got us some legitimate businesses. Everything she once had on us has no validity anymore. We made sure of it."

But even after they sorted shit out, they didn't come for me. They waited for me to come to them, and that really does hurt.

I absently rub my chest, which suddenly feels tight. "I don't even know what to say right now," I admit, looking Mom in the eyes. "But I know I never want to see you again, you disgust me, and you're right. I don't have a mother."

I storm into the clubhouse, straight to Saint's room, where I dive into his bed and cry.

Fuck everyone.

Chapter Seventeen

About ten minutes pass before Saint quietly slips inside and closes the door behind him. He slides into bed next to me and pulls me against him, kissing the top of my head.

"I'm so sorry, Sky. I didn't know the truth of what happened back then either, but then Hammer finally admitted it to me the other night. I told him he had to tell you. He's right, it's fucked up, and I can see why he never wanted you to know, but now at least the truth is out there. I think you're right to be angry. I'm so fucking sorry this happened. Now you know why we never fought for you and why they broke up in the first place, and it might just sound like a bunch of excuses, but fuck. I'm just sorry, okay? If I could do it over, I'd do it differently."

I don't know what he means by that exactly, but I don't ask. If he means that he'd go against the club's wishes and come for me, it's best that he not say it out loud. It doesn't change anything anyway. It's all done, and now I just need to decide what I'm going to do with all this new information.

"Maybe Hammer was right—ignorance is bliss. I don't think this wound is ever going to stop hurting," I admit, wiping my eyes. "I just don't understand how someone could even suggest doing that to their own flesh and blood. I don't get it. She never loved me, Saint, and that proved it. She said she never trusted me, but I never did anything to her."

"She's crazy and jealous," Saint tells me, rubbing my back in soothing circles. "You can't expect rational thought from her, and you did nothing wrong, Skylar. She is the number one person meant to protect you, but she only cares about herself. Good fucking riddance, I say. Georgia is something else."

Great, I win the worst mother award. "Fuck my life," I whisper, taking a weak moment to just feel sorry for myself. "I don't want to see her ever again, Saint."

"She won't be stepping in here again that's for sure," he says, kissing my temple.

"What happened to the rival MC president? Hammer is obviously not dead, so did he just give up?" I ask, wondering what happened to the war between them.

"Killer got put in prison," Saint explains. "So no retribution happened. Not that he would have been able to kill Hammer, but he would have tried. And we would all have to watch our backs every second of every day."

"So it all worked out in the end."

For everyone except me.

She loved Hammer more than she loved me. I don't know why that hurts, because if I'm being honest I loved him more than I loved her too, but I'd never hurt her or throw her under the bus. I wouldn't do that to anyone, never mind my own flesh and blood. Saint is right—she's clearly not right in the head, or maybe she is just pure evil.

Drying my tears, I look at Saint and gather all of my strength. I'm here right now, and I'm fine. I'm strong. I don't need that woman, I guess I never did.

I can't change what has already happened. I'm going to do something with my life. I'm going to thrive, and I don't need anyone in my life who isn't going to cheer for me, celebrate with me, and just simply love me.

Everyone else, blood or not, is being left behind.

"I have to admit, I didn't see that one coming," I admit, closing my eyes and taking a deep breath. "At least it's all out in the open now. I hated not knowing what had happened, and why you or Hammer didn't even try and contact me."

"Hammer and I actually got into a fight over it," Saint admits, pushing my hair back off my face. "I didn't understand why we were letting Georgia dictate our actions. I was pissed. But Hammer said it was the only option for now, and before we knew it you would be eighteen and could do what you want. He said you'd come back to us."

"And what if I hadn't? Would you have come to me?" I ask him. "Because I'm a little older than eighteen, and you only reached out to me when you were locked up."

"Because it made me think about what was important in my life," he says, wiping away a tear from my cheek. "I didn't know who you were anymore, if you wanted to talk to any of us after what had happened. I didn't know much. Yes, we kept an eye on you from afar as best as we could, but we didn't really know all the details of your life." He sighs deeply.

I ask the question that I'm not ready to hear the answer to yet. "Would you have done what Hammer did? Would you have put the club before me? Would you do that now?"

"Things aren't always as easy as you make them sound, Sky."

"They are to me," I whisper, feeling uneasy by how noncommittal that answer was.

He holds me closer, and eventually, I fall asleep.

When I wake up in the morning I jump in the shower and replay last night in my head. I can't let this affect me or my life—I need to feel the pain and then let it go.

Mom would want me to feel weak, helpless, and maybe even run back to her, but I'm not going to do that. I might not have been a perfect daughter, but no one deserves a mother like that one, and when I have children I'm going to make sure I'm nothing like her.

Saint opens the glass door, seeing me naked for the first time. I don't cover myself up; I let him have his fill, the look in his eyes making me feel sexier than ever.

I ask, "Do you want to join me?"

He nods and undresses, and I realize he was waiting for an invitation. I have to set the pace, not him, and I know if I told him to leave, he would have. I get distracted as my eyes land on his body, such masculine perfection.

He steps under the scalding hot water, but doesn't complain as he puts some bodywash on his hands and starts to massage my shoulders. I close my eyes and let him, enjoying the touch and the pampering. "How are you feeling?" he asks, tone husky.

"Better," I whisper, then clear my throat. "I'm not going to let her win. Yes, it's shitty and she's shitty, but now I just have to keep moving forward and try not to let her impact my life at all."

I can only control *my* actions. I can't give myself the mother I always wanted, but I can let go and move forward and not use her as an excuse for anything.

"She's a twisted woman," he mutters, now rubbing

my back. "But you're nothing like her. At all. And I think that's why she has a problem with you, because she knows you're better than her. You're kind, and smart, and witty, and we all fucking adore you."

Smiling sadly, I turn around and look up at him. "I just want to pretend last night never happened. Just for a little bit."

Cupping my cheek, he drops his head and starts to kiss me, pushing me back against the tiles. "I think I know a way I can distract you."

"Go on then," I manage to get out, watching as he drops to his knees in front of me, water dripping down his skin.

"Now I know you said you're a virgin," he says, lifting my thigh up and around his shoulder, so I'm balancing on one leg up against the wall. "But just how innocent are we talking? Has anyone ever tasted you here?" he asks, running his finger along my sex.

Swallowing hard, I shake my head no.

"So I'm going to be the first to taste this sweet pussy?" he asks, flicking his tongue out and licking me once before delving in a little deeper, sliding his tongue inside me.

"Yes, you're the first," I tell him, watching his head bob up and down as he starts to lick and suck on my clit. "Holy fuck."

I've never felt anything like this, and watching him pleasure me is so sexy. I couldn't look away if I tried. My thighs start to tremble, my breaths turning into pants.

I brace my hands against the tiles to hold me up as pleasure hits me. "Okay, wow, you're really good at that," I mutter, unable to help the moans that escape my lips.

Saint starts to laugh a little at my narration, and I don't know if I should feel offended or not. Is it normal to laugh during this? I forget my train of thought as the pleasure starts to get more intense, building with each second, until he makes me come, and my thighs are trembling, shaking with the power of my orgasm's intensity. He doesn't even stop then, not until I push him off me, gasping for breath.

Saint stands, his giant erection looking right at me, begging for attention. I want to give him what he gave me, even though I've never done it before. However, I have watched a few instructional videos on it.

Still, I feel a little shy, especially thinking about all the experienced women he must have been with. But then watching him, knowing how much he wants me, is a confidence boost, and I feel comfortable enough with him to explore and test the waters a little.

Reaching out, I begin to stroke him, watching him get even harder in my hand. His penis is really big and thick, and I honestly have no idea how that is going to fit inside my mouth, or anywhere else.

"Saint?"

"Hmmm?"

"Why do you have to be so big?" I ask him, making him chuckle under his breath, eyes darker than ever on me. "I'm serious. I'm pretty sure this isn't normal. It's like the size of my forearm."

Hesitating, I move to my knees, which embarrassingly happens to make that cracking sound, and explore him a little more before tasting the tip and twirling my tongue around him. "Well, that's better than I thought it was going to be."

More laughter, this time choked.

Taking the head into my mouth, I swirl my tongue around him again, getting the taste of him. Then, feeling a little bold, I try to take as much as I can down to the back of my throat, but my gag reflex kicks in and I push him straight out. "I think I need a little practice."

"Sky, you are doing fine," he murmurs. "Just you touching me and looking at me like that is about to have me explode, trust me. There's nothing you can do that is wrong or will turn me off."

"Okay," I say, then continue to suck, tease and lick, getting into a rhythm and figuring out what he likes by his moan and body language. When his fingers tighten in my hair, I know he's loving what I'm doing. I continue to suck and tease until he's about to explode, and when he does he stays true to his word and pulls away, coming all over my breasts while I watch in fascination.

"Fuck," he whispers, face a mask of pleasure. It's a good look for him, and one I plan on seeing many more times in the near future.

He washes me off once he's finished, and we scrub ourselves again, this time to actually get clean before we get out.

"I liked that," I say as he wraps a towel around me. "I wonder what your come tastes like."

He makes a choking sound. "Fuck's sake, Sky. If you don't stop you're about to find out."

"You can go again so fast?" I ask him, staring down at his cock, which is hardening. "Oh…my."

But I pretend I can't see it, because I'm kind of hungry and need to sate my other desires now.

"Do you think someone ate our food?" I ask, making him laugh out loud.

Chapter Eighteen

Hammer's at the breakfast table, and I start to feel extremely awkward when I think about what I was just doing under his roof.

"Good morning," I say to him, turning the kettle on and then sitting down.

"Morning. How are you?" he asks, brow furrowing in concern. "Your mom left straight after and I told her not to ever come back or she's going to regret it."

"Thanks," I say, smiling sadly. "I'm okay. Much better than last night, anyway. I'm glad I know the truth, but I can see why you didn't want me to know. It's pretty damn fucked up."

"Understatement," he says, reaching out and touching my arm. "We've got you, all right? You're my daughter, I don't care what your birth certificate says, and I don't want to lose you again. I love you, Sky."

"I love you too… Dad," I say, realizing that I've started calling him Hammer instead of the usual Dad. I don't know why, I guess I'm still figuring out where the hell I stand here. "And I'm not going anywhere. But I have to admit, I'm a little hurt about the whole thing."

"I understand," he replies, glancing down at his hands.

"You chose protecting the club over me," I whisper,

swallowing hard. "You say you love me and that I'm your daughter, but you were willing to let me go with her, knowing what she was capable of."

I hold up my hand when he tries to speak, because I need to say what I have to and get it off my chest. "It's true that she never hurt me or anything like that, but you didn't know that. And I wasn't in a loving environment with her. She just tolerated me, and I took it because she is my mother and the only person I had left. I knew she didn't really love me the way a mother should. But I always thought you loved me like a father should. But I can't help but feel like you didn't. You picked a club over me—that's something I expected from her. But not you."

"I'm sorry, Skylar," he says, sounding sincere. "The men rely on me to protect them, and if Georgia fucked us over that would have been on me. I brought her here, and I trusted her at one point. Which was a huge mistake. I couldn't let her hurt the club, all that I have built, and possibly get us arrested and put away. However, I should have found a way to keep her off our backs and still have kept you. I'm so sorry, Skylar. When things settled down, I should have come for you. I didn't know if you'd want to see me, or what lies Georgia had been feeding you. I was a fucking coward. But don't you think that because I let you go with your mom that I don't mean it when I say I love you, because I do. I thought about you a lot, and I fucking missed you, and—"

I lean over and hug him, cutting off his apology. He hugs me back, squeezing me tight. "I'm sorry," he says again into my hair. "It's hard being the president, but it's even harder being a dad. And I fucked it up."

What happened will always hurt, but I know I'm going to forgive him. It's either that or walk away, and that's not going to happen. I love the man, and he's the only parent I have left.

"I forgive you, Dad," I tell him, pulling back and smiling.

He looks me in the eye. "I will never put anything before you again. Please believe me when I say that. I got your back and I don't want to lose you again."

"I know."

He smiles in relief, and stands up. "Good. I don't know what I'd do if you didn't. I'm not going to let you down again, Sky."

He makes me a coffee just as Saint comes in. "Did they eat the food from last night?"

"I didn't check." I smirk, watching him while he does.

"Seriously, you can't leave food anywhere in this house," he grumbles, scanning the contents in the fridge.

"I'll have a mango," I tell him, and thank Hammer for the coffee.

I start to think about what i'm going to say to Logan about this whole thing with Mom. I know I need to tell him and the rest of my brothers, but it could end badly. What if he says that she would never do something like that and doesn't believe me? Or maybe he will take my side. I don't expect him to, though. This is my battle, my war, and i'm not going to make my brothers choose.

Saint slides a cut-up mango in front of me. "Thanks. Do you want to go for a ride or something? I just have to be home in the afternoon so I can get ready for work."

"You haven't quit yet?" Hammer asks, frowning. "I thought you were going to."

"Not yet," I tell him, eating a piece of the fruit. "My paramedics program starts in a few weeks, so I'm going to keep working and make some money. And no, I don't want any of your money. You're doing more than enough for me as it is."

"You enrolled?" he asks, sounding surprised. I remember then that Mom showed up just as I was about to tell them all, and I only ended up telling Saint later that night. "I'm so proud of you, Sky. Congrats. You know you don't need to work, though, right?"

"Yes, I do," I fire back. "I've always worked; I don't even remember a time when I haven't worked. It's all I know. And I like working, I'm not a lazy person."

"You think I don't know that? I just want to make your life a little easier, especially when money isn't an issue for any of us," Hammer says, looking to Saint. "Your man here is loaded too. If you don't want to take my money, take his."

Saint smirks at me and raises his brows. "She's going to be stubborn about it. There's no point trying to convince her—she's just going to say no for the sake of it now."

My eyes narrow on him. "That is not why I'm saying no. I'm saying no because it's my life and I get to choose how I want to live it." I pause, before adding, "Not that I don't appreciate the offer. I just want to make my own money, not take it from someone else like some... I don't know..."

"A kept woman?" Saint suggests, while Hammer says, "Spoiled little daddy's girl?"

"All of the above," I say with a laugh. I don't know how the hell I'm even able to laugh after everything.

Maybe I've lost my damn mind at this point.

But could anyone blame me?

After lunch and a long ride with Saint, I head back home and run into Logan just as he's coming in from work. "You look tired," I say as he unlocks the door.

"Working in the sun is a killer," he admits. "I was helping fix a fence." He lets me enter first. "Did you stay at the clubhouse last night?"

"Yeah, and guess who dropped by," I say, placing my bag down on the kitchen counter.

"Who?" he asks.

I wait a few seconds to make it extra dramatic. "Mom. She came to tell me that if I didn't leave with her, she's going to disown me."

Logan's jaw drops open. "Mom came to the club-house? With Neville?"

"No, she came alone. Unless he was waiting for her in the car. She probably told him she had to run in and drop something off for charity or something," I add in a dry tone.

He snorts, knowing that it is probably something our mother would do.

"And that's not all. Everything came out, about why Hammer and her split up, about how she didn't want them contacting any of us, especially me."

"So what happened?" he asks, which sobers me as I realize I'm going to have to tell him everything.

I start at the beginning of the night, and don't miss out details. By the end of it, my brother is fuming. I don't think I've ever seen him this mad in my life.

"Are you fucking kidding me? Tell me this is some sick joke, please!" he yells, pacing. "I knew she was crazy, but that is something else. How the fuck did this woman birth us?"

I jump up on the counter and sit there, watching my legs dangle. "I don't know. Apparently she's only re-ally terrible to me because she wanted another boy." Telling the story again stirred all those feelings from last night. There are tears in my eyes. I hope one day it will hurt less.

"I'm so sorry, Skylar," he says, coming to stand in front of me. "I'm not going to have anything to do with her anymore. That is…" He trails off, shaking his head. "Despicable. What kind of person does something like that?"

We talk a bit longer about the whole thing, and he wants to call our brothers. I give him permission to fill them in, but I can't bear to hear or retell the story again, so I head up to my room. I know they say blood is thicker than water, but in this case that's not the truth. Betrayal from your own blood is painful.

When Saint's cousins come back at my work that night, I figure this must be their local. "Hello," I say to them both. "How are you?"

"Good," Daisy replies, showing off the huge diamond on her finger. "Brad proposed! After only six months! Can you believe it? And look at the size of the rock."

"It's a huge rock," I admit. After chatting with them for a little longer, I realize why Saint isn't that close to them. I almost feel like the two of them should have their own TV show where they get to talk about themselves and how much money their men have spent on them recently.

I'm about to excuse myself and get back to work when Jamila says something that gets my attention. "I hope Thorn brings Tory to the engagement. It's been ages since we've seen her."

Tory?

I want to ask them who the hell Tory is, but they're acting like I should already know, so maybe it's one of

Saint's ex-girlfriends. He hasn't mentioned any of the previous women he has dated, so I have no idea what his history is like. He's acting like I'm his first real relationship, like he is mine, but I doubt that is the case. I make a mental note to ask him about this, and about Tory specifically, the next time I see him.

"Maybe he will come to the next one?" I lie, smiling at them both. "I better get back to work, but you both have a good night, and congrats on the engagement, Daisy."

"Thank you." She beams, lifting her ring up at me again, just in case it didn't blind me enough the first time.

The two of them head to the dance floor, and I look over at my manager, who is smirking at me. "How do you know those two?"

"They're Saint's cousins," I admit, shrugging. "He's not that close to his family, so I only met them for the first time the other night. They come here much?"

She nods. "Yeah, I see them here a lot. They spend a shit load of money on drinks, that's for sure."

"Yeah, but whose money?" I mutter.

She laughs out loud. "Not theirs. But stupid men's money is still money."

"Ain't that the truth? Hopefully it picks up tonight," I say, glancing around the mostly empty bar. "Or is this what we should come to expect on a weeknight?"

"It will pick up," she assures me, carrying some clean glasses over to the counter. "Everyone comes here after the casino, usually."

"Just a casual night of gambling and drinking."

"Yep," she laughs.

"My best friend, Max, is the guitarist and lead singer

of a band—I could get them to come and play here, if you're interested?" I ask, doing a quick search on my phone and showing her a video of them. It would be good to get Max more exposure, and also another reason for him to come visit me.

"Hey, I've heard of these guys," she says, nodding. "We'd love to have them here. We're pretty booked up for the next month but after that, hell yeah!"

"Awesome, let me know what date, and I'll see if they're free."

The place soon starts to fill up, keeping me busy for the rest of the night.

However, my mind is on Saint, and whoever this Tory is.

Chapter Nineteen

"Have you seen that hot chick who lives near the club-house?" I overhear Renny ask Temper as soon as I step outside, looking for Saint. "Her house is the closest one to us. She's fucking sexy."

"Nope, but you should probably stay away from her. Don't shit where you eat. Or even down the road from where you eat," Temper replies, glancing up as he notices me. "Hey, Sky, what are you up to? Did we miss any more family feuds?"

"Nope, just that final battle," I say, dropping into the chair next to them. "Where's Saint?"

"He went to grab some shit from the store," Renny explains, offering me one of the beers from the six-pack he's holding. "Whenever he knows you're coming here he goes and buys aisle four for you."

"Thanks," I say, accepting it and opening the lid on my T-shirt. "What can I say, a girl's gotta eat."

"Don't know where it goes, though," Temper adds, downing half his beer in one mouthful.

"When are you going to settle down?" I ask Temper in return, watching, amused as he starts to choke on his beer. "What? Is the concept that foreign to you? Don't you want a wife and kids?"

"Never met anyone worthy of making her my old lady," he admits with a shrug. "I'm not the easiest man to deal with, Skylar."

"You're nice to me."

"You're a kid," he fires back. "And you're family. You see a different side of me that not many get to see."

I consider his words. "Okay, so if you did meet someone you liked, you could show her that side too? You aren't getting any younger. And yes, that was payback for the kid comment."

He chuckles at that. "I haven't been on a date in five years, I think it is now. I don't think the whole dating thing is for me. I'm old school. And not just a few decades ago old school—more like caveman."

"Even cavemen brought women home to their caves," I point out.

He nods sharply. "Yeah, by hitting them over their heads."

I laugh, but he doesn't. "Okay, well, maybe don't do that."

Renny laughs out loud from beside him. "He's a little psychotic. But I wouldn't have anyone else at my back."

"Don't think that's on top of a woman's checklist these days," Temper says to us both. "None of the pretty ones are asking for a man to cover their back while they are doing shady shit."

"Are the non-pretty ones asking for that?" I ask, confused. "I'm sure there are some pretty criminals out there that would love that about you, Temper. But maybe you should go for a nice woman. Someone with quiet strength. Maybe she could balance you out a little."

"Why aren't you giving Renegade any shit about

this?" he grumbles, finishing his beer and placing the empty glass bottle down on the table.

"Because he was talking about some hot chick when I walked in, so he's still in the game," I point out. "You I've never heard talking about any woman."

"I'll talk about one when I have something nice to say about one," he declares.

Saint walks in, and Temper eyes him in irritation. "Thank fuck you're back. Your girl here is giving me relationship advice, and I'm not drunk enough yet to deal with that."

Saint leans down with a cheeky grin, and kisses me longer than he should in front of company. "I'm sure she has some good advice for you, Temper. Come on, Skylar, I'm going to cook for you, just like I told you I would."

I remember what he wrote in the letter, smiling as he pulls me to stand up and leads me to the kitchen.

"You shouldn't poke Temper, you know," he says, lifting me up on the counter. "I know he's nice with you, and calm, but I've seen him flip the fuck out. Don't get me wrong, I'd take him on if he ever directed that at you, but I'm just saying be careful."

"I've heard that about him," I admit, remembering Hammer giving me a similar warning. "I don't know, I feel safe with Temper. I don't think he'd ever hurt me."

"You feel safe with all the monsters," he grumbles, getting a frying pan out of the cupboard and placing it on the stove. "How was work last night?"

"It was good," I tell him as he starts to get busy in the kitchen. "Your cousins were there again. What are you making, exactly?"

"Spaghetti," he says, turning to look at me in excitement. "A do-over for the shitty one I made you years ago. And yeah, they go out a lot, those two. They consider themselves socialites."

"Daisy has a huge rock on her finger," I tell him, and then linger a little before trying to casually drop the question I've been meaning to ask him. "And they mentioned that you haven't been to a family function since the last one you went to with Tory."

He fumbles in his onion cutting, then pauses for a second before continuing.

"Who is Tory? Is that your ex or something? You haven't said much about anyone you've dated and…" I trail off, waiting for him to chime in with answers.

"No," he replies, dragging out the word. "I've never brought a girlfriend home to meet my family. I haven't really had any serious girlfriends aside from one, and that never worked out." He turns around and glances at me. "You have nothing to worry about, Skylar."

"You didn't answer the question. Who is Tory then?" I ask, narrowing my eyes. A bad feeling settles in my gut, something not sitting right with me.

With a sigh, he pulls out his phone from his pocket and presses a few buttons. I'm about to yell at him when he walks over and shows me a picture.

"This is Tory," he says, a little hesitantly.

I glance down at the little girl with bright blue eyes and a cute, dimpled smile. She is beautiful, the poster child for the perfect baby girl, and looks to be about two years old.

"This is Tory?" I ask, confused.

Until it hits me.

I do a double take of those blue eyes.

"She's yours?" I ask, breath hitching. "You have a

daughter? And you didn't think it was a good idea to mention that?"

My voice gets higher with each word, until I'm yelling loudly. I'm sure the whole clubhouse can hear me.

"It's complicated," he says, glancing at the picture himself, then sliding his phone away. "And I didn't want you to walk away because you knew I had a child with someone else."

"So what, you were just going to bring her to our wedding one day and yell surprise?" I ask, standing up and stepping closer to him, being confrontational. I'm hurt, and I'm sick of feeling this way. It's like when it comes to me no one can be honest. They all care more about how they feel and what's best for them. But no one stops to think about me. In the end I'm left feeling betrayed, *every damn time*. So much has happened recently and I've shared all of that with him, and he didn't feel the need to be open and tell me about this? I just don't understand.

"And what's complicated exactly, Saint? Because the only thing that's complicated for me is the fact that you purposely didn't tell me this huge bit of information. I've been talking about honesty, communication. We even discussed having children in the far-off future, and you didn't think any of those times were good enough to bring up the fact that you already chose to have a child with someone else?"

Saint grabs my shoulders and gets me to look at him. "I didn't choose anything. She got pregnant—it was an accident. She was on the pill, but forgot to take it."

These things happen, I know. But he could have been more responsible.

Thorn Benson, the love of my life, has a child with another woman. And he lied about it.

I don't understand why he lied to me. He could have told me about Tory in his letters, or when we first saw each other again. He could have told me, but he specifically chose not to. This isn't a small deception. And then there is the other thing…

He has a child. While he's been my firsts for everything, my first kiss, my first lover, and one day I thought the father of my children, I was none of those to him.

I wasn't his first kiss, his first lover, and I didn't give him his first child.

"You saved nothing for me," I whisper, feeling empty all of a sudden.

"I saved *everything* for you," he growls, eyes scanning mine. "I never gave anyone all of me, no one, and even if I wanted to, I couldn't. Because deep down inside, I knew that I was meant to be with you, and no one else. I would never make anyone else my wife, Skylar. I've saved that for you."

Nothing.

"Skylar, are you listening to what I'm saying?" he asks me, cupping my face, begging me to look at him.

I keep my eyes on his chest, because I don't want to look at him anymore.

I can't.

He's a liar.

First my mother, and now him.

Is there anyone I can trust?

Chapter Twenty

Hammer steps into the kitchen, looking at us both like he'd rather be anywhere else but felt like he should check up on me.

"Are you okay?" he asks me, brow furrowing.

I turn the heat on to him. "You obviously knew Saint had a fucking child, and you didn't think *I* should know about it? How come no one can just tell me the truth, straight up, as it happens? Why does no one think about my feelings first? You're *my* father."

"Sky—"

"I'm the last person to know everything, and then I get some bullshit story about not wanting me to get hurt. Well, guess what, guys? Lying to me, it hurts! Being kept in the dark, yeah, that hurts too. And having to hear from two women in a bar that the man I thought was my fucking soul mate has a child, yeah, you guessed it, that also fucking hurts. So save me any speeches the two of you have, because I'm leaving."

Hammer blocks the door with his large build. "I told Saint he needed to tell you. That was up to him, not me, Skylar. The two of you are in a relationship, and it's between both of you. And it's a complicated situation with Tory. I'm sure if you let him explain—"

"I'm not listening to shit," I state, hands on my hips. "I get that it's between me and him, but you know what I've been through recently! How much more shit am I going to have to take by the men who claim to love me?"

I turn to face Saint. "It doesn't matter what explanation you have—you had your chance, many chances I might add, and you still didn't tell me about it. You have a real fucking problem with communicating, and you are still so closed off with me. You say I'm the only one you want, that we have a connection that has lasted years of separation and change, then why won't you let me in?"

Hammer steps aside, and Saint follows after me as I make my swift exit to my car. When I open the door and get in, he sits in the passenger side.

"Please leave. I do not want to speak to you at the moment, so please get out of my car," I growl.

He stays silent for a few seconds.

"I don't know if she *is* my kid," he says quietly. "My ex, if you can call her that, we slept with each other only a handful of times. She told me that Tory wasn't mine a year after she was born. For that whole year I spent so much time with her, loved her, and spoiled her, and then Carol decided to drop that on me."

That…was not what I expected. I don't even know what to say to that. While I'm still angry over finding out about the child in the first place, I can't help but feel awful at what he's telling me now.

Confusion also fills me. Why is everything so complicated with this man?

"I didn't not tell you about Tory because I wanted to keep it from you. I didn't tell you because I don't talk about it, or her. I haven't seen her in months, and I'm just fucking pretending everything is fine when it's not, because I don't know what the hell is going on. And yeah, I miss my little girl. My little girl who apparently isn't even mine. And I'm sorry I didn't tell you."

He pauses, letting his words sink in. "Yes, there was an element of it that I didn't tell you because I thought you would get angry or walk away from me because it was too much to handle. No one wants to deal with baby mama bullshit, and no one wants to find out that the person they want to be with has a child already with another woman. Skylar, you put me up on this pedestal, but I'm not perfect. This isn't some forbidden romance story. I'm just a man, a biker, and yes, I've been with a lot of women over the years, and maybe even knocked one of them up. But I never loved them. I love you, and I always will."

He reaches out and touches my face. "I love you, Skylar. Don't give up on me, not just yet, okay?"

Swallowing hard, my heart breaks for everyone in this situation.

For him, for not knowing if the daughter he loves is his.

For Tory, who hasn't seen her dad and must be missing him.

And for me and my teenage dream that Saint would be mine and mine only, and when I finally had to share him, it would be with our own children. It might sound petty and unrealistic, but I do feel saddened about this.

"Maybe I *have* put you on a pedestal, or maybe my expectations are set too high, I don't know, but I never, ever, for one second thought that you would have gotten another woman pregnant," I admit, being a hundred percent honest.

"Sky," he whispers, ducking his head, like my words hurt him.

Well, his actions have hurt me, so I guess we are even.

"I know that sounds stupid and immature. But you just sprang this on me and it's a lot to process. And unlike some people—" I give him a glare "—I want to be honest in how I'm feeling, no matter how foolish my thoughts are. I can be mature about this and admit that part of my anger is unjustified, but—"

"You have nothing to feel stupid about," he tries to assure me, cutting me off. "This was before you, Sky. You can't be mad at me about something that happened before we were together. There's nothing wrong with having high expectations—fuck, you deserve the world—but can you judge me for my actions now, not what I've done in the past?"

Closing my eyes, I rest my head back on my car seat, sighing deeply. "I *am* judging you for your actions now. You never told me the truth, Saint."

"I knew it would upset you."

"That doesn't give you a free pass not to tell me," I quickly reply.

"I'm fucking this up," he whispers. "I love you, Sky. I'm beginning to think I always did, even when I forbid myself to even go there. I'm sorry, all right? And I know it seems like I'm always fucking apologizing, but I'm trying. I'm going to do better, and I'll be more open and honest."

Saint is trying to love me.

But he needs to try harder if this is going to work.

"I love you, too, Saint. I always have," I say, opening my eyes and turning to him. "I'm sorry about the situation with Tory and her mother, but yeah, you should have told me."

"I know."

Half of me wants to help him sort out the situation and be there for him through it, and the other half of me just wants to be selfish and make it about me. Right now, I just want to go home and cry, and feel sorry for myself because although I'd never admit it out loud, my perfectly constructed future has been shattered.

It's so ridiculous that I feel this way, so I think I need to cry it out. I need to vent to Max, even though I know he's going to tell me that I'm overreacting and I need to get over it.

Saint just hasn't let me in emotionally, and how can we move forward if he isn't going to?

"I'm all in in this, Saint. I moved here and found you. I'm here right now, for you," I say, feeling emotional, my voice breaking a little. "And now I'm here, and you're saying all the right things, but you have this irrational need to protect me from everything that will hurt me, even though I need to know it. It's not fair."

I hold up my hand when he's about to speak, stopping him. "I do not need someone to protect me. I need a partner who will be my equal and who will respect me."

He's silent for a few second before he speaks. "You're right. And you know what? If the roles were reversed, I'd hate it. I'd be furious. I'm not as open as you are, but I'm trying to be. It doesn't come naturally to me, but I'm willing to work on it for you. I'll do whatever I have to to make this work. I'm so fucking sorry I didn't tell you the truth."

If Tory is Saint's—and going by her eyes, I think she is—she is a part of him. This isn't about me, and wouldn't be my perfect plan for us, it would be about loving Saint's kid like I would my own, because I do love him.

"Sky, can you please say something?" he rumbles, and glances at the door. He wants to leave too.

How is this going to work if we can't communicate properly? It's way too soon for us to be having these concerns; we should be in the honeymoon stage, not fighting about issues way too big for me to handle.

I open my mouth to say I want to go home, and we can talk about this later, but I know that if I do that Saint is just going to close off even more from me. I need to show him he can trust me and that I'm not going anywhere unless he lies to me about something or betrays my trust again, because there's no coming back from that. Yes, I want to make this work, but I'm not going to be treated any less than I deserve. I can forgive him this time, but only a fool would a second time.

"I won't be lied to again, Saint," I say, looking him in the eye, expression blank. "I deserve honesty from you. And I will give you that in return, that and more. I know you only trust your MC, but you also used to trust me, and I need you to get back to that place where you aren't scared to tell me something because you think I will run away, or that I can't handle it. I *can* handle it." Not that I expected something like this to come up.

"I should have told you," he agrees, taking my hand in his. "I just… I knew you'd be disappointed."

That's an understatement. I think it was more of a shock than anything. I honestly didn't see it coming, and I just wish I had gotten to hear it from him. I don't think I'm a hard person to speak to, and I don't understand what he was thinking when he decided not to tell me. It was always going to come out; it's like he was just buying time.

"It doesn't matter what my reaction is—you still need to be honest," I whisper, staring down at our now joined hands. I've romanticized my relationship with Saint so much, but the truth of it is exactly what Logan was trying to tell me. I'm going to have be stronger to be in a relationship with him than with just a normal guy. Not that they don't do things like this either, but with Saint so much more can be tested.

Everything is going to be put on the line.

The question isn't how much I can handle, it's how much *will* I handle.

Chapter Twenty-One

"How are you, Sky? I miss you," Max says, putting on a sad voice.

"I miss you too," I say into the speakerphone, rolling over onto my stomach on my bed and resting my face on my palm, legs in the air. "There's been so much going on here, I really wish you were here right now."

"Is everything okay?" he asks, sounding concerned. "Your room is still empty here if you decide you want to come home."

"Saint has a kid. Or, well, he maybe has a kid," I blurt out, rolling over onto my back and staring up at the ceiling.

Max is silent for a few seconds. "And how do you feel about it?"

"Honestly?"

"Always."

I bite the inside of my cheek. "Disappointed. He never even told me about her. I had to find out for myself."

"Okay, how would you feel if he just told you straight up about his kid?" he asks.

I think about it. "I guess I'd still feel a little…surprised and kind of let down, but I wouldn't question our relationship over it. Him hiding it just makes me wonder what else he is hiding or chooses not to tell me."

"Yeah, the lying thing is pretty sketchy. I think you have every right to be upset over that aspect."

"Good, I needed to hear that," I admit, taking a deep breath. "Things just weren't meant to be this way."

"So what are you going to do? You do love kids, though. You're great with them. You know every time there was a crying baby or toddler having a tantrum in the café, you were always the one we sent in to help," he says, chuckling softly. "I know that it's not ideal, but you'd be great around any kid, never mind the child of someone you love. I don't think you have anything to worry about." He pauses, then asks, "Or is it the fact that you aren't the one he waited to have kids with that's the real issue here?"

"It's not that he didn't wait for me," I explain. "I didn't expect him to wait; that's unrealistic. We didn't even know if we'd see each other again, and we weren't even dating or anything romantic before. I guess it's just not how I thought we'd ever be. Saint thinks I've made up unrealistic expectations and put him on a pedestal, and now he feels like he has to live up to my idea of him."

"Maybe you have? You just said you didn't expect him to wait for you, and I'm sorry, but in case you didn't know, having sex can sometimes equal babies," he says, whispering down the line like it's some big secret. "It happens to the best of us."

"Hasn't happened to either of us," I point out.

"You're a virgin and I'm not stupid," he says, chuckling to himself again.

"See! You just called Saint stupid."

"I did not," he says, laughing harder now. "Look, sometimes shit happens. You can think you are being a hundred percent safe, and a baby still happens. The only way to guarantee not getting someone pregnant is to not have sex. And we all know your man—and I, for that matter—are not going to not have sex."

Now I'm laughing. "You're right. I know you're right. And yes, when you put it that way it seems ridiculous to be upset over something like that."

I know I can't hold on to this. I need to forgive and move forward, or if I can't accept things, I need to walk away. It's not fair for me to pretend to forgive him but then bring it up at any opportunity. At the end of the day I need to think rationally, and although it hurts—and boy does it—he didn't betray me. It has nothing to do with me, really, and maybe that is what hurts the most. I wasn't here, and what he did or got up to, and the decisions he made, had nothing to do with me.

But keeping the truth from me, though—that part hurts and I can't pretend it doesn't.

"Like you said, you love him. So don't be petty and hold grudges, Sky. I know you. For someone so sweet, you can hold a grudge worse than anyone I know. No one is perfect," he says.

"You're right," I say, still not ready to let this go.

Max sighs heavily. "Let's do a little role reversal here. Let's say you got pregnant out here in the country. But then you reconnected with Saint years later. How would you feel if he was upset and mad at you for getting pregnant with someone else's kid when he was never in your life during that time?"

Shit. When he puts it that way, I feel like a complete idiot. If roles were reversed, I'd feel horrified if he were mad at me for something I couldn't control or change. Leave it to Max to put things in perspective.

"You shit. Okay, okay. You're right. I'll let it go," and

when I say it, I mean it. I need to move on and not throw this in his face again. I am not my mother; I refuse to be manipulative and petty.

"Good. Can we talk about me now?"

I laugh hard. "Okay, tell me about you. When is your next gig? Who are you dating? And most importantly, when are you coming to see me?"

Talking to Max makes me realize how much I miss him. We speak for another hour and when we hang up, I feel lighter, and see things much clearer.

That's the power of a best friend.

Saint picks me up from Logan's in his car the next afternoon, and tells me he has a surprise for me. I know with all the tension between us recently, we do need some alone time together to figure it all out. Now that I've calmed down and thought about everything, I want to try to see where his head is.

"So where are we going?" I ask as we pass the street that leads to the clubhouse.

"Surprise, Sky," he replies, flashing me a cheeky grin. "But you're going to find out in about thirty minutes."

"I'm intrigued," I murmur, glancing out the window. We haven't really spoken properly since he got out of my car the day before, just because I wanted a little time to reflect on everything. It's nice that he's putting in effort; he obviously wants to sort everything out just as much as I do. It's not a nice feeling when things are all up in the air and you don't know where you both stand. "We're heading half an hour out of town?"

"You're asking too many questions," he teases, nodding to the glove box. "I put some snacks in there for you for the ride."

"Are they to keep me quiet?" I tease, opening the compartment and pulling out a few of my favorites: chocolate, pretzels and marshmallows. "Because it's probably going to work. Man, I'm going to get so big the longer I hang around you."

"You'd be beautiful no matter what size you are," he replies as I rip open the wrapper on a chocolate bar.

"Do you want a bite? It's the least I can do after that little comment," I say, grinning and offering him the first one. He takes a chunk out of it, almost half the bar, leaving me staring down at it. "You have a big mouth."

"The better to eat you with, my dear," he mutters, making me laugh out loud. I remember the shower and how he made me orgasm, and other thoughts enter my mind. I can't wait until I get to be with him like that again.

"Yes, you are pretty good at that," I say, chewing and swallowing. "I guess you being experienced comes with its perks."

"I'm glad you see it that way," he replies, trying to keep a straight face. "You always could see the silver lining in everything, glad to know that hasn't changed."

"Well, there's no point being bitter about everything. That's hardly a way to live your life," I say with a shrug.

I'm on to the marshmallows when we pull up to a place in the middle of nowhere. "What are we doing here, Saint? Because this looks like a place someone would stop at to dispose of a body. I'm ride or die and all, but I don't know if our relationship is ready for burying a body together."

He laughs and gets out of the car, so I do the same, following him to the trunk. He takes out a tent first.

"We're going camping?" I ask, glancing around the deserted grounds. It looks like it could be a camping site, but there's nobody here except us. "Are we allowed to camp here?"

"Better keep our clothes on so if we aren't we can run back to the car," he jokes, pulling everything we could possibly need from the back of his car—blankets, pillows, food, the whole nine yards—then starts to set up while I watch. He leaves the car lights on so he can see.

"Do you want any help?" I ask, hoping he doesn't take me up on the offer, because I've never put up a tent in my life and have no idea how to do so.

"I'm good," he calls out, chuckling under his breath.

I pop another pink marshmallow into my mouth, then realize I should save them for s'mores tonight. "Okay, if you're sure."

He doesn't take long, and soon we have our own little glamping setup, with a blowup mattress and warm, thick blankets inside the tent. He even put a little welcome mat at the front. When he pulls out a portable gas stove, my jaw drops open.

"Done this before, have you?" I ask, impressed by his preparation and the effort that goes into sleeping in the wild.

"I love camping. I asked you about it once, and you said you've never been but wanted to go one day," he tells me, and I smile because he did remember. "Did you end up going?"

"I did actually, once," I admit, lying down on the mattress and watching as he does the same. "Max wanted to go for his birthday one year, but we stayed on a camping grounds so they had showers and toilets. Speaking of, where are we going to shower and go to the bathroom?"

"There's a lake down that way," he says, pointing

to the right. "But we will head back tomorrow, so I'm sure you'll survive if you skip a shower for one night."

Luckily I had one this morning, but I usually have one every night as well. "And the toilet?"

"In the woods," he says casually, grinning at my re-action. "If you need to poop, I will dig you a hole."

I blink slowly a few times. "There's no way in hell I'm pooping in the bush, in the middle of nowhere, with you nearby."

"You'll change your mind if you really need to go," he says with confidence. "This is going to be a bonding moment for us."

I roll closer to him, so our noses are almost touch-ing. "No amount of bonding will let you see me poop."

He laughs at me and pulls me closer. "I love you," he says, kissing my lips. "I felt so shitty after you drove off, and I know a lot of what you said is true. I can be closed off, and from now on, for you, I'm going to be an open book. Nothing is off limits, and everything you ask will be answered, brutal fucking honesty and all. And I'm going to assume that anything I tell you won't make you run away."

"Good," I say, reaching out to touch the stubble on his cheek. "And I thought about a lot too, and I want you to know that whatever happens with Tory, I'm going to be here for you and support you."

"Thank you," he says, the relief in his voice evident.

"Why don't you get a DNA test done once and for all so you can find out for your peace of mind?"

"You'd really be okay with that?" he asks, studying me, as if making sure I'm being honest. "I haven't re-quested the DNA test because if she's not mine I don't know what the fuck I'm going to do. But you're right, something has to give and I can't just live in limbo like this forever."

I nod. "Yeah, I mean, I don't know the situation with her mother, but whatever you choose I'm going to be right here next to you. I agree, I think you should find out the truth."

"Carol is…difficult to deal with. She does love Tory, and I mean, she's not the worst mother, but she won't hesitate to use her as a weapon to get what she wants either. I don't mean to be a walking fucking stereotype right now, and I know that most men say this about their exes, but she is crazy."

"How so?" I ask, brow furrowing. "Like 'wants money, gold digger' crazy, tries to fight any woman she sees you with, or stalker type?"

"All of the above," he admits, cringing and rolling onto his back, staring up at the roof of the tent. "Well, maybe not the stalker part, but everything else. We were never actually together, we were just casually fucking, and…" He trails off, scrubbing a hand down his face. "I want to say yeah, I fucked up, but then Tory wouldn't be here. So it's a hard situation. Basically Carol said she was protected, and we were using condoms anyway, but then one time…" He glances over at me. "Do you know how fucking hard it is to speak about this to you? You, of all people."

"It's hard to hear too," I admit, taking a deep breath. "But it's our reality, so keep going."

"She told me she was pregnant and it was mine. We didn't get together after that, but I made sure she was looked after, gave her money and went to all the appointments and everything with her. I might not have loved her, but that was my child inside her and that meant something to me."

"As it should," I whisper.

"Tory was born and she was just a bright light, you know? I loved her the moment I saw her, and I told myself I'd do whatever I could to be a good father. Then a few months ago Carol told me I'm not even the father, said it was the man she's with now." He sits up with his knees to his chest. "And then I went out and got drunk, and lo and behold, the fucker was also there. He's the one I hit and got arrested for. He pressed assault and battery charges. I was facing at least three to five years minimum."

"Then how'd you get out in less than six months?"

"My plea deal was for a year. But, I don't know, overcrowding or some shit," he explains, shrugging. "My lawyer is one of the best, and he knows his shit. Carol hasn't been in contact, and I haven't seen Tory in months. I know you're right, I need to figure out what I'm going to do, because I just can't pretend this whole thing doesn't exist anymore. I miss her. And it breaks my heart that she's probably thinking this other douche is her dad, because he's living with them now and taking on that role."

"She has your eyes, Saint," I tell him quietly. "When I saw her, I knew she was yours straight away, and if she is, you need to fight for her."

He turns to me, and lies back down, facing me again. "Fuck, I love you so much, Skylar. I know this isn't what you would have wanted—"

I cut him off, shaking my head. "It doesn't matter. I was being selfish. This is a little human we're talking about, and it was wrong of me to think of her as ruining some epic love story between us that I've created in my head these last few years. But you not telling me about her, on the other hand…"

"We can still have the epic love story," he says, rolling me onto my back with him on top of me. "We just might have a little princess with us now and again. And it will only be honesty from here on out."

"I'm okay with that," I say, looking into his eyes. "Like you said, she's a part of you, and I love all of you."

He slams his lips down on mine, kissing me deeply, but slowly. Hungry kisses that let me know I've made the right choice and that things are going to be okay.

We are going to be okay.

Chapter Twenty-Two

Glancing up at the clear night sky and the stars, which are so visible tonight, with a warm campfire in front of us, I whisper, "Now that is a view." I love being here, and can't wait to spend the entire night with him like this. We're all alone, with not a soul in sight, and with the fire going it's a beautiful atmosphere. "Thank you for bringing me here tonight, Saint. I'm really enjoying myself."

And I've decided that tonight is the night.

I want Saint to make me his. I want him to be my first.

"Me too," he says, eating his marshmallow off a stick. "I think I really needed to get away, and even more than that I needed some alone time with you. You know I'm never going to give up on you. No matter what, I'm going to be here, fighting for you, fighting for us. So in the moments you don't believe in us, I'm going to believe in us for the both of us."

My eyes widen at the stark sincerity in his tone.

"Thank you, Saint," I say, moving closer. "I adore you, you know that, right?"

"And I fucking adore you," he replies, lifting his blanket up and pulling me under it. We cuddle up together, just lying there for a little while, enjoying each other's company before Saint cooks dinner on the portable stove, frying sausages and onions to eat in a bun.

"Hot dogs under moonlight, who knew this could be romantic?" I tease after we finish eating and pack up everything. Except now I need to pee, which I've been holding in for a little too long. "Can I have the flashlight?"

He hands it to me. "Do you want me to come with you?"

"No," I say, staring out into the darkness. "I won't go too far."

"Call me if you need me," he murmurs, amused, while I traipse into the woods armed with nothing but a flashlight and some toilet paper. I go behind a tree and pull my pants down, do my business and stand back up.

I'm about to pull up my pants when I feel something the size of my palm crawling on my leg, so I start to scream, "Oh my God!" picturing some huge ass spider on me and shaking my legs, before running toward the camp.

Pants falling back down to my ankles, I end up tripping over and land on my face.

"Ouch."

Just great.

Lifting my head, I dust my face off with my hands, grimacing at the sand.

Of course Saint finds me lying there, and helps me up. "What happened? Are you okay? Are you hurt?"

"Something crawled up my leg," I admit, as he pulls my pants up for me and fastens them. "It was probably a killer spider. This is how it ends for me, Saint."

"Did you actually get bitten? I told you I'd come with you," he sighs, dusting some more sand off my face. Lifting me up in his arms, he carries me back to the camp where I wash my face and hands. He checks me for bites, but there's nothing there. "Do you want to go for a swim in the lake?"

"To drown the spider that's potentially still on me? What's in there?" I ask warily.

"No idea," he replies a little too cheerfully. "And there's no spider. It was probably a leaf or something. The water will probably be freezing, but we can clean ourselves up."

Considering when we were sitting around the fire I decided I want to have sex with Saint tonight, freshening up probably isn't the worst idea. "Yeah, I guess so."

We walk down to the water hand in hand, and Saint undresses me, chuckling before doing the same for himself.

"What's so funny?" I press.

"You, lying there on your face." He laughs out loud. "I knew I should have come with you. I thought maybe with all that time in the country, you'd become a little more accustomed to nature."

I open my mouth, then close it. "I don't like bugs. No amount of country living is going to change that."

He pushes my hair off my face, chuckles dying down. "You're so fucking beautiful," he murmurs, running his hands down my arms and the sides of my body. "How did I get so lucky?"

Something hard pokes me in the stomach. "Wow, you're really happy to see me."

"Ignore it," he replies, amusement lacing his deep voice. "I know I am."

I dip my toe into the icy water and shiver. "Fuck me dead."

Saint mutters something under his breath, but I don't catch it. "What did you say?"

"Nothing," he replies, laughing softly. He splashes some water on him, washing his body and brushing his teeth, and I do the same, then wrap myself in a thick towel.

"Surprisingly refreshing," I mutter, glancing up at the moon. "It's a full moon tonight. Doesn't that make people crazy?" Seth told me that his girlfriend told him that nights with a full moon are crazy at the hospital, and the weirdest shit happens with the most random and over-the-top medical encounters.

Saint lifts me in his arms like a bride and kisses me. "I don't know. I guess if you believe in all of that shit."

I cuddle against his chest. "Tonight has been so fun. Even if I had to pee on the ground then fell over on my face with my pants around my ankles. Not my finest moment."

"At least you didn't knock yourself out or something, because the closest hospital is back in the city," he rumbles, kissing the top of my head. "You're a menace, you know that?"

"I'm not usually such a damsel in distress, I promise," I add, grinning to myself. "But I guess I do have my *Knight* in shining armor now."

Saint pauses in his steps. "Did you just make a Knight pun?"

"I did, and how great was it?" I ask, wrapping my arms around his neck.

I can't remember the last time I felt this carefree. Saint and I are good, I've made a decision in regards to my future career path, and I don't have to worry about my finances and whether I'm going to make rent this week or not. I have a family who loves and supports me.

Hammer is back in my life, along with all the men in the MC, and… I'm happy.

When Saint puts me on my feet, I drop the towel on top of my clothes and turn to him, pressing my palm against his soft, smooth chest and tracing the tattoos there. When I glance up at him, he must see the hunger in my green eyes, because he makes a deep sound in his throat and cups my face kissing me deeply. His towel drops, and we press our bodies together, skin on skin. He leads me backward and onto the blowup mattress, our lips never leaving each other's.

It's not long before he starts to trail his lips down my body, and gently spreads my thighs. I start to get excited knowing what's coming, something I've been craving since we had that shower together, but I want more from him this time.

I want everything.

"Yes," I whisper, as Saint kisses up my thighs, teasing me and turning me on even more. He has me arching my back, silently begging him for more as he kisses my inner thigh, nibbling the sensitive skin there. Goose bumps appear on my flesh, my nipples pebbled to the point of pain.

By the time he puts his mouth on my pussy, I'm all but begging for it, so turned on that I can't even think straight. Using his talented tongue, he brings me to ecstasy by licking, sucking and eating me. My thighs start to quiver, my breathing so heavy anyone would think I'd been running in a marathon. He makes a growling sound in the back of his throat, letting me know that he's enjoying it too, which is so sexy to me. I didn't even know men enjoyed going down on a woman, but Saint has shown me otherwise.

He pays special attention to my clit, running the tip of his tongue over it repeatedly, but just before I'm about to come he stops and raises himself over me, rubbing his cock against my entrance. I'm so on edge, and so needing to come right now.

"Are you sure, Sky?" he asks me, sounding gruffer than I've ever heard him.

"Yes, I'm sure," I reply, breathless. "I want you, Saint."

He gets up and pulls out a condom from his bag. I'd give him shit for being so hopeful, but I'm just glad that he's prepared because I'm not on the pill just yet.

After ripping the condom packet open with his teeth, he rolls it down his length and returns to the position he was in before, stroking my clit and then gliding the tip of his finger inside me, touching my wetness, before slowly sliding his hard cock inside me, inch by inch.

He sucks my nipple, sending pleasure through me. At the same time there's a little bit of pain. He stills, waiting for me to get used to him before he starts to move. It feels so good, the pleasure so much more than the slight dash of pain.

"Are you okay?" he asks, tone husky. I look into his eyes and see so much there. Heat, pleasure, and concern. He doesn't want to hurt me, but little does he know he's making this an experience for me that I'm never going to forget.

I nod. "I'm fine. More than fine."

Then I kiss him, deeply, my fingernails scoring down his back.

I finally see what all the fuss is about.

Suddenly, he pulls out of me and puts his mouth back on my pussy, licking me over and over until I come, his name on my lips.

Only then does he slide back inside me, thrusting gently, kissing me, letting me taste myself.

When he comes I love watching him, looking into his eyes and seeing the desire there, listening to the sexy growling sounds he makes, which only turns me on further. After he's finished, he rests his forehead against mine and kisses my lips.

He then lies back next to me, breathing heavily, and silently reaches out his pinky finger to touch mine. "That was…"

"Worth the wait," I finish, rolling closer to him and resting my head on his chest. I feel a little sore, but in a good way, and I know he made it the best for me as possible, his experience paying off once again.

"I fucking love you," I think I hear Saint whisper.

I fall asleep with a smile on my face.

Chapter Twenty-Three

For the first time since getting this job, I start to feel a little uneasy about two men at the bar. It's not like they have been unruly or overly rude or anything, but I just don't like the way they are looking at me. It's almost like they're studying me, or memorizing me, and it's making me feel really uncomfortable. They both grin at me, and then at each other, and something about them makes me nickname them Dumb and Dumber in my head.

"Hey, sweetheart, can we get another one?" one of the men asks, even though my manager is closer to them.

"Sure," I reply, forcing a smile and making another two gin and tonics. After I deliver them, I take my break in the staff room, not wanting to be around the bar until they leave. Checking my phone, I find a few messages. Three are from my mother. All the same.

Sky, I'm your mother. You have to talk to me eventually.

Why are you being a little brat about this?

Can you call me? Can we talk about this?

I ignore them all and read the message from Max.

Got a gig in the city next weekend, so I'll see you then! I'll send you the details.

"Yes," I cheer to myself, typing back a quick reply. Something to look forward to.

Can't wait to see you! I'll make sure I have next weekend off. You still need to play at my work too!

Lucky for me, the men are gone by the time my break is over and the atmosphere is back to normal. An hour or two later I see a familiar face, bringing an instant scowl to my expression.

"Seriously? Tell me Saint or Hammer didn't send you here," I ask Dee, crossing my arms. Every time I see Dee now, my guard is up. He reminds me of being babysat and spied on at a time when I had no idea the MC had any kind of involvement in my life. I know it's not his fault, he was just following orders, but the sight of him sets me on edge.

He puts his hands up in submission. "Calm down, feisty one. I'm actually here on a date. She suggested the place. Don't worry, my time following you is over. I've moved onto bigger and better things now."

"From spying on women in bars to going on dates instead?" I ask him, arching my brow. "Do you want a drink? Or maybe I should be offering your date a drink instead." She's the one who has to put up with him for the night.

"I'll have a beer. You know, Sky, I think you and I got off on the wrong foot. I was following you because Hammer made me, yet you're still angry at me but not him. How is that fair?"

The man has a point. "Okay, I guess you're right. Every time I see you now I just assume you're here being a spy, and I'm sorry."

"I appreciate that," he replies in a dry tone. He places some money down on the table and eyes the busy dance floor. "I should probably message her and tell her that I'm here."

"Where did you meet her?" I ask, wondering what his type is going to be.

"Online," he replies, flashing me his teeth. "Is there any other way these days? We can't all meet our true love in a clubhouse."

"Yeah, I don't think love is really what they're distributing out there," I agree, laughing out loud. I notice that Dee has taken the time to dress up and is in a navy blue shirt with his hair slicked back. "So what is Dee short for? Derek? Damion?"

He starts laughing, loudly. "No, my real name is Wade."

"Why do they call you Dee then?" I ask, grabbing the beer I almost forgot to get him, and taking the money from the counter. "Because you can be a dick?"

"Closer," he replies, glancing at his phone. "Okay, she says she's here and wearing a white dress."

Nosy, I glance around, trying to spot anyone with that description. "Over there," I say, pointing to this girl sitting in one of the corner booths. "Good luck."

"I don't need luck," he says with a cocky wink. As he turns around to go to her, he bumps right into another woman, and she spills her drink down his shirt.

Oops. I grab a cloth and hand it to him over the bar. "Are you sure you don't need any luck?"

If looks could kill.

Miss White Dress spots Dee and makes her way over

to him. "Wade?" she asks, voice soft and feminine. She's beautiful, with blonde curly hair and a full figure.

"Yes," he murmurs, turning to face her. "Nice to meet you, Maryanne."

Feeling like I'm a part of the first date awkwardness, I want to move away, but I can't seem to make myself, instead glancing between the two of them and eavesdropping without shame. Dee has forgotten about his alcohol-soaked shirt, now lost in Maryanne's eyes, the two of them seemingly taken with each other.

"Can I get you a drink?" he asks her, placing the cloth back down on the bar.

"I'd love one. A tequila sunrise, please," she says, smiling up at him like he's her prince charming.

"Tequila sunrise, please," he echoes to me, before turning his attention back to his new woman.

I make her drink and place it on the table. "That's fifteen dollars, thanks."

He gives me his credit card this time, and it's true his name is Wade. Wade Simpson, actually. No D in his surname either.

Swiping the card, I look up at him and sigh. "Oh no, your card declined."

"What?" he asks, glancing down at the eftpos machine and then at Maryanne, surprise written all over his expression. For a moment, I consider playing this out, but it is kind of mean, so I relent.

"Just kidding," I smirk, handing his card back to him.

"I'm going to kill you," he mutters under his breath.

"Now, now, Dee, don't be showing your true self on the first date—she will run," I reply quietly, laughing and moving to serve another customer.

The rest of the night goes quickly, and Dee says bye before he leaves with his date.

Wrap your willy, I mouth to him. He simply shakes his head at me and pulls Maryanne outside as fast as he can.

Saint picks me up from work on his Harley, and he truly looks so sexy on it. The bike is black, and he's dressed in all black too—jeans, leather jacket and biker boots. He removes his helmet and jumps off, coming toward me as I stand out front of the bar, under the moonlight.

"The night I've had," he growls, scooping me in his arms and dipping me backward with a kiss. "I've missed you."

"I missed you too," I reply, holding on to his neck. "What happened?"

"Just some shit with the club," he says, giving away nothing. "It's been a long day and all I want is to be in bed with you next to me." He pauses. "Or on top of me."

"Well, we better get you home then," I reply, grabbing my helmet off the back of his bike and putting it on. After I get on behind him I squeeze him tightly and feel his stomach.

Yeah, I can't wait to be in bed with him either.

"So I messaged Carol and told her that I want to do a DNA test," Saint tells me as we're naked in bed after a very long session of showing each other how good it felt to see one another. He's running his finger up and down my arm, sending goose bumps all over my body.

"Not my idea of pillow talk, but go on," I tease, kissing his shoulder. "Did she agree?"

"No," he replies. "She didn't, which makes me think she has something to hide, or doesn't want a certain outcome. But I spoke to a lawyer, a good family lawyer at the Bentley and Channing law firm. I can get a court-ordered DNA test, so I'm going to do that."

"Good," I whisper against his skin. "I'm glad you're going to fight for her."

I don't know why this woman has decided to punish Saint, but I can only guess. He most likely ended things with her or she saw him with another woman, something like that to make her turn spiteful and put her needs above her child's. Or maybe it's the truth and she's not sure who the father is. I guess everything will come out with time.

"As long as I have you by my side, I can fight for anything," he replies, tracing my lips with his thumb. "Thank you for being the angel on my shoulder, Sky. I think you've always been that for me."

"Thank you for loving me like you do," I reply, kissing him on the lips. "I'm sure it will all work out for you. Maybe Carol will come around and let you see Tory in the meantime."

"She might. There's only one thing she loves other than her daughter, and that's money. I could try offering her some money if she lets me see Tory once a week or something."

"You shouldn't have to pay to see your own child. I mean, you already do pay child support, right?" I ask him.

"Yeah, I pay child support for her. Which I should tell Carol she can kiss goodbye if Tory isn't mine," he adds, frowning. "Pretty shitty how that works out, isn't it? Some men don't even get to see their kids but have to still pay, by law. The system is fucked. If Carol is determined to keep Tory from me, I know I'm not going to win in court. I can use the court for the DNA test, but if it came down to a custody battle, they'd take one look at me and I'd lose. I'm a biker, I'm covered in tattoos, I'm big and I've recently been to prison for assault."

"We'll worry about that when we get to it," I tell him. "Let's just get the DNA test sorted, and maybe you starting to see her again. I'd love to meet her."

"I'll try make it happen," he agrees, nuzzling my head. "I never choose the easy route, do I? It's always something, and I know I've fucked up with my choice of baby mama, and I'm sorry I'm dragging you into this with me."

"It is what it is," I say, yawning. "You don't have to keep saying sorry. We will handle it all together." He squeezes me tighter. "Oh, and Max is visiting next weekend, so me and him are going to catch up. He's doing a gig here—do you want to come with me? You can meet him."

I feel Saint stiffen a little, so I open my eyes and look at him. "He's family to me, and one of my closest friends. Don't act all weird just because he has a penis, because trust me, friendship is all we have, and is all we will ever have."

"You really think heterosexual men and women can be friends, and just friends?" he asks me. "Usually one person wants to fuck the other, who is friend zoning them. I don't think I've ever met a guy and girl who are just genuinely best friends, with a purely platonic relationship. Usually someone secretly has a crush. Unless you grew up together or are childhood friends or something, maybe."

"You're so cynical. Just because you don't have any female friends you don't want to fuck, doesn't mean that other people don't," I fire back, feeling a little annoyed at his comments. "I've been friends with Max for years, and I think I'd be able to tell if there was a little something more there for either of us, but there isn't. We're basically like brother and sister—we give each other shit, and I could comfortably be around him in any situation."

"Don't get angry at me, I'm just telling you what I think," he grumbles, lifting my hand to his mouth and kissing the back of my palm. "All right, if it means that much to you, I'll meet this guy, and I'll be on my best behavior."

"He's the one who was there for me, Saint," I tell him, my stern tone letting him know how important this is to me. "He held me together, and that means something to me. So please don't be weird about it. He's important to me and I want the two of you to get along."

"Okay," he agrees. "I'm hearing you, Sky. Relax."

Melting back into him, I hope he keeps to his word, because the last thing I need right now is more drama.

I think I have my fair share as it is.

Next weekend comes up fast, and soon I'm pushing through a crowd of women screaming and loving Max and the band. Saint is at the bar, ordering us a drink. I was hoping to catch Max before his set began, but we ended up running late because Saint and I ended up in bed together, almost like he was reminding me that I'm his or something—as if I need the reminder.

"Max!" I call out, wanting him to see that I'm here.

"Max is mine," some girl next to me says, elbowing me out the way.

"You psycho," I say, elbowing her back and glancing up at the stage to find him waving at me.

"You know him?" she asks, suddenly my best friend. "He's so dreamy! Can you introduce me to him?"

"Fuck no," I reply, heading back to the bar and away from the crazy-ass fans he's accumulating the more popular his band gets.

"It's a warzone out there," I say to Saint as I reclaim my seat next to him. "I almost feel sorry for Max." If I didn't know how much he loves the attention.

"Their music is pretty good," Saint admits, sliding my cocktail my way. I can't stop looking at him in his white shirt tonight. He looks sexy as hell, and since he usually wears black it's something different.

"Yeah, they are amazing," I agree, bringing the margarita to my lips and taking a sip.

"This song is one I wrote for my friend, Skylar. Skylar, this one is for you," Max calls out, making me almost spit out the liquid in my mouth.

Saint throws me a look, one that clearly says *I told you so*, but when Max starts singing it has nothing to do with anything other than him being friends with a girl who is funny, loyal and loves to give him shit all of the time.

"If I needed to be brought back down to earth, she'd be the one to do it..."

The song seems to be about him climbing the ladder to fame, and about me being the one who helped get him there, which is very sweet of him. As Saint listens to the lyrics, he loosens the hold on his glass, which was about to crack in his hand, and relaxes a little. I don't know how I'd feel if a woman wrote a song about Saint, and I can't believe that Max wrote one about me. It's very nice of him, but I wish I was given a heads-up about it. I was trying to make a point to Saint that we're just normal, close friends, and a song isn't working in my favor right now, even if it is just about a close friendship.

"See, just a friend saying thank you to another friend," I point out, taking a casual sip of my drink.

"He has some balls, I'll give him that," Saint growls, then turns to me with a fake smile. "Just a friend saying thank you."

I laugh at his expression. "I love *you*, Saint. You have no competition in this whole world. You could send me anywhere, with the hottest men on the face of this earth and it wouldn't matter. I'd still choose you, every single time."

Blue eyes soften. "I'd choose you too, Skylar. No matter what."

"Good," I murmur, lifting my glass up. He clinks his against it. "To us, forever."

"To us," he says, our eyes locked as we drink once more.

We turn our attention back to Max and enjoy the rest of his songs.

When they take a break, Max comes straight to me and gives me a giant hug. "Fuck, man, it's so good to see you, Sky."

"You too, Max," I say, smiling at him. "This is Saint. Saint, this is Max."

Max turns to Saint and smiles widely, offering him his hand. "Nice to meet you, man. I've heard a lot about you."

"All good things, I hope." Saint grins, flashing his teeth.

"Yep, all good. Except the whole baby mama drama, but hey, you can't win them all right?" Max says with a casual shrug. Saint laughs, while I cringe and down the rest of my drink.

"Come on, I'll order us a round," Max says, slapping Saint on the shoulder.

Saint flashes me a look that says "he's not so bad after all" and the two of them get talking.

Almost makes me feel like the third wheel after a while, but as long as they aren't killing each other, I'm happy.

Chapter Twenty-Four

"What the hell is going on in here?" I ask Saint as we step into the clubhouse a few nights later. All I can hear is music, cheering and laughter. After just having a night out with Max, I didn't think I'd be attending another outing so soon. "Are they having a party?"

"It's Renny's birthday today," he explains, closing the door behind us.

The scene I step into makes me laugh out loud. Renny is sitting there, blindfolded and in nothing but a pair of boxer shorts, and there are two women in front of him, feeding him cake.

"What birthday party game is this? Whatever it is, Saint, you aren't playing it," I declare, glancing around at the giant happy birthday sign and the balloons. There are two cakes on the table, so I step forward and grab a piece. "Who made the cake?"

Saint chuckles and wraps his arms around me. "I don't know, but I think he's blindfolded because he has to choose which cake tastes better without looking at it."

"So the women are here as cake models?" I ask, brow furrowing.

"This is Renny's party after all," Saint reminds me,

and yeah, it does seem like something Renny would appreciate.

"Maybe we should have invited the woman next door he has a crush on," I say, taking a bite of the chocolate cake. "Do you want to party with them? I can go home and sleep," I ask him, not minding. Saint and I have been spending so much time together, I'm sure he would love some time with his brothers without me there, and I'm totally fine with it. Women around and all.

"No, they're going to be drinking all night, and I want to take you to your first day tomorrow," he replies, leading me away from the laughter and toward his room.

Tomorrow is my first day in the paramedics program, and I can't wait to start this new chapter. Over the last few weeks everything between Saint and me has been amazing—we've been communicating more and just talking about everything, and he has really opened up to me, which I'm grateful for. I think even Logan is coming around now, especially after I brought Saint in to talk to him and meet Sabrina. I haven't heard anything else from my mom, so I guess she's sticking to her word about disowning me, but it's peaceful now, and I'm not upset about it anymore. My life is better without her in it. She's a toxic person, and although it's sad, it's just how things need to be. Sorting out my schooling was the final part I needed to make my life exactly how I want it, and now that I'm here I'm never looking back.

"Are you sure?" I ask as we enter his room, and I drop down onto his bed, kicking off my shoes, removing my clothes and climbing under the sheets. "Or you can leave me here to read a book and fall asleep."

"I have a little something more interesting than reading a book—"

"You obviously don't know how good this book is," I cut him off, teasing.

He takes off his shoes and shirt, standing there in a pair of low-slung jeans and a smile. "Can't be more interesting than this."

He slowly undoes his belt and then pulls down his jeans, his cock straining against his briefs. Arms folded back behind my head, I lick my lips and watch the show as he takes it all off, standing there naked before me.

When he starts to stroke his length up and down slowly, then faster, I sit up and crawl toward the end of the bed. On my knees, I take over the job for him, using my hands and then my mouth to pleasure him. He gets harder the second my mouth is on him, and his fingers tangle in my hair, encouraging me.

When he starts to get impatient, he steps out of my reach and comes around to the bed, lifting me up and tossing me back against the pillow. Lips slam down onto mine, kissing me while he rubs his engorged penis against me, and every time he slides against my clit I can't help but moan a little, lifting my hips, begging for more. He pushes inside me, just the tip at first, then the rest of him.

"Saint," I whisper, nibbling on his ear.

He lifts his head up and looks at me. "Yes? You feel fucking amazing."

"So do you," I say with a smile, cupping his face and bringing it back down for me to kiss. Going on the pill was the best decision ever.

He pulls out of me and turns me over onto my stomach, lifting my hips up and sliding back into me in one smooth thrust. At the same time he reaches between my legs to stroke me there. He's so generous in bed—

he never makes it just about him, and I know that every single time he's going to make sure I'm satisfied, the mark of a true gentleman.

My nipples rub against the bed with each thrust, adding extra sensation. He kisses the back of my neck, sending shivers up my spine, and I'm so wet I can literally feel how damp I am, wetness spilling out onto my inner thighs.

"Fuck," I moan, as he gently pulls my hair back, turning my head to the side to kiss me. He lets go of me and grips my hips, sliding in and out of me in a slow grind, while I push back against him.

I bite down on the pillow as he makes me come, and seconds later he follows me, finishing inside me.

He pulls out and lies back, grabbing me and spooning me, his chest moving up and down. "See, much better than drinking with the men."

The men choose to laugh loudly at this exact moment, and we can hear them all the way from outside.

"Are the walls really thin, or is it just me?" I ask, wondering how much they can hear.

"Is that why you suffocate yourself with a pillow when you come?"

"Yes," I reply, laughing. "I don't want anyone to hear me, especially Dad. That's traumatizing. For both of us."

"But I love hearing you and the little noises you make," he admits, biting down gently on my neck. "You are so sexy, you know that?"

"I do now," I reply, rolling over and getting as close to him as I possibly can. "And thank you for making me feel that way."

Don't get me wrong, I've always had a healthy self-esteem, but with Saint I just feel beautiful, wanted and loved all the time. It doesn't matter what I look like, whether I've just woken up or I'm all dolled up, he always looks at me like I'm the most beautiful woman he's ever laid his eyes on.

"I love you," he whispers, tucking my red strands back behind my ears. "Are you excited for tomorrow?"

I nod. "Yeah, I am. Feels good to finally have some direction and a plan, instead of just being flaky and hiding behind random jobs."

"Does this mean you're going to quit the bar?"

"No."

"Stubborn," he says with a head shake. "I'm going to make you an additional cardholder for my credit card, so if you need anything, just use it and I'll pay it off."

"Why the hell would you do that?" I ask him, lifting my head. "That's so unnecessary. Dad is already paying for me to do this program, and I don't need you paying for anything for me either."

"Sky, it's not a big deal," he replies, brow furrowing in confusion. "Just keep it for emergencies if you're feeling weird about it."

"Saint—"

"Stop being stubborn," he says, interrupting my rant. "Choose your battles, Sky. I read that somewhere. That's what relationships are all about, choosing your battles. I feel like this one isn't one you should pick, because I'm just trying to look after my woman a little, even if she doesn't want me to or need me to."

I open my mouth, then close it. "Okay, I'll save my battle for something else, then."

He's right, he's just trying to take care of me, even if I prefer to be more independent and not expect anything from him. It's not like I *have* to use the credit card. If it makes him feel better, there is no harm in accepting it. I know that some women specifically look for men who will do this for them, but I'm not one of them. I don't need lavish gifts or lots of money to make me happy, but I can appreciate the fact he wants me to have a backup in case of emergencies.

"Good girl," he replies, grinning at me. "Look at us, not killing each other and compromising."

"I just compromised, actually," I state. "And I hope it's going to be reciprocated at some point soon."

He kisses me, stopping me from saying anything else. "You have a smart mouth."

"You love it."

"And I have compromised already. I didn't say anything when you went to go hang out with Max all alone. Even though I don't love it, I know he means something to you, so I stay quiet and don't give you hell over it."

Yeah, he didn't love it, but he just told me to call if I needed him and message him when I got home safely, which I appreciated.

"You're right," I reply, grinning. "You've been toning down the whole alpha overprotective bullshit, and I appreciate it. Anyway, I'm going to jump in the shower—would you like to join me?"

He responds by getting out of bed and picking me up, carrying me to the shower.

So much for toning it down.

Chapter Twenty-Five

I see Carol from a distance before I see Tory, the little girl standing next to the swing set at the park. She's a pretty, petite blonde, pretty much the total opposite of me. Maybe Saint doesn't have a type, or hell, maybe I'm not even his type at all. It's been a week since he requested the DNA test, and suddenly Carol is playing nice, being flexible and letting Saint see Tory whenever he wants, but of course it comes with a price.

He squeezes my hand, bringing me back to reality. Today is about meeting Tory, and nothing else. It's not time for me to start feeling insecure, or questioning things because I'm finally getting a look into his life before I came back.

"There she is," he murmurs, and my eyes drop to the most beautiful little girl ever. Her dark hair is in pigtails, and she's wearing a pink dress with gold strappy shoes.

"Tory!" he calls out, and the little girl spins and looks in our direction. When she sees Saint, her blue eyes light up and she runs over to him.

"Daddy!" she calls out in her baby voice, holding her little chubby arms out. Saint picks her up and gives her the biggest hug.

"How are you, Tory?" he asks her, kissing her cheeks.

"Good," she replies, beaming up at him. "I good, Daddy."

Saint turns to me and steps closer. "Tory, this is Sky. Can you say Sky?"

"Sky!" she calls out, giggling.

"Nice to meet you, Tory," I say, smiling.

Carol walks over, and up close I can see that life hasn't always been kind to her. She looks tired, her face weathered and worn. I don't know if she's just much older than Saint, or if maybe time hasn't worked in her favor.

"So, you're the new flavor of the month," Carol remarks, eying me.

"So you're the woman using her child as a weapon," I fire back, my temper getting the better of me. I regret it as soon as the words leave my mouth, both because Tory is present but also because I should be the bigger person and just not say anything, because she's just not worth any of my time or energy.

"That's enough, Carol," Saint says to her, holding on to Tory. "I'll bring her back in two hours, like we agreed."

"Did you put the money in my account like *you* agreed?" she asks, pursing her lips.

"Yes, the money was transferred."

We walk back to our car, and the whole time I can't help myself from judging Carol, and even judging Saint for sleeping with her. Forget looks or anything else— Carol is obviously not a nice person. She has no dignity or self-respect and is blackmailing Saint for money to see his kid. Also, if she were so certain Saint wasn't Tory's father, why would she still let her see him?

Out of all the women Saint could have been with and gotten pregnant, why did it have to be this one? I know he says Carol loves Tory, and that might be true, but it can't be healthy for Tory being raised by this woman. Although I could be still grappling with my own mother issues and projecting onto Carol and Tory.

I don't verbalize any of my thoughts—it's not going to help the situation in any way—but that doesn't mean I'm not thinking it. Saint puts Tory in her car seat and the two of us get into the car, a weird tension between us.

"Did we decide on where we are going to take her?" I ask, turning on the radio.

"How about the aquarium?" he suggests, reaching out and touching my thigh. He lowers his voice so only I can hear. "Don't listen to anything Carol says. You know what you are to me."

"I know. And I'm sorry for engaging with her. I'll be better around Tory."

The situation is far from ideal, but it's not my situation to fix, it's theirs. All I can do is try to be there for Saint, and to put in effort with Tory and try to be a good role model whenever I'm in her presence, which means no more snarky remarks from me, no matter how much Carol tries to bait me.

We go to the aquarium, and Tory's face lights up when she sees the starfish and the turtles. I don't know much about two-year-olds, but she seems very clever.

"Pretty," she says, and I turn around thinking she's talking about one of the starfish again, but she's looking right at me. She reaches out from Saint's arms and touches my hair. "Pretty hair."

"Thank you," I say to her. "You have pretty hair too."

She giggles and puts her arms out, trying to come to me, so I let her all but jump into my arms. As she buries her face into my neck, Saint and I look at each other.

This isn't what I ever would have asked for, but with this little girl in my arms I feel like I don't even care if Saint is her biological father. She's his.

And she's perfect.

After class I head straight to the clubhouse. "This has been the best week ever," I tell Saint, Hammer and Temper, who are sitting outside chatting. "I'm so happy I decided to do this." I love going to class every day, learning all these new skills on saving people, and it's just such an empowering feeling. I stop my rant when I realize something isn't quite right, going by how tense the men are.

"Is everything okay?" I ask. I must have interrupted some club business, or some other conversation that stopped the second I made an appearance.

"It's fine, Sky," Hammer says, reaching out to touch my hand. "I'm glad you found your calling. It makes me happy seeing you happy. And soon you won't have to serve drinks for a living." He turns to Saint and smirks. "And now because you have a man, I don't even have to pay for it."

"What do you mean?" I ask, confused.

"Saint paid for it. Didn't he tell you?" Hammer asks, glancing between us.

"No, I didn't tell her, because I knew she was going to give me shit about it," Saint mutters, throwing Hammer a dirty look.

Hammer simply shrugs. "He's your man and he wanted to pay for it. Don't need my bank anymore when you have his."

Fuck's sake.

This program was a hell of a lot of money, but I didn't feel that bad about Hammer paying for it—he's my dad and has paid for and bought many things for me growing up.

But Saint paying for it? That's different.

"I'm going to pay you back," I announce to him.

"See?" Saint growls.

"At least she's not a gold digger like the last one," Temper adds, chuckling to himself.

Pursing my lips at that comment, I turn to Saint but before I can open my mouth he starts talking. "Sky, you don't need to pay anything back; don't be ridiculous. You just study and then save some lives."

"Some biker lives," Temper adds. "You're basically an investment."

I throw my hands up in the air. "I can't deal with the lot of you, seriously. But Saint…" I turn to my man. "I can't thank you enough. You really didn't have to do that."

"I wanted to," he replies, brushing it off. He lowers his voice and says, "I don't know what you think we're doing here, Sky, but I'm in this forever. That means we're going to look after each other and support each other, and that's what I'm doing."

I feel a little bad that he didn't even want to tell me because he knew I'd have something to say about it, but it's not that I'm ungrateful. I don't ever want him to think that. It's just that I don't like feeling like I owe someone.

"Thank you," I say, kissing his stubbled cheek. "I appreciate it."

"I know you do," he says, leaning in and pressing his soft lips against mine.

"Okay, get a room, you two," Temper adds, looking uncomfortable. "I don't know where the fuck to look right now. How'd you deal with it, Hammer?"

Dad just shrugs. "At least she's with a Knight. Imagine her bringing some banker or businessman home. This way she's here almost every fucking day and I get to see her."

"I'd come and see you anyway," I point out. "Are you sure everything is okay?"

I can tell when it's not, because the change in atmosphere is so obvious.

"Yeah, just club business," Dad replies, glancing up and flashing me a smile, as if to reassure me.

"Okay," I reply, lips pursing. I know they aren't going to tell me anything else, so I change the subject. "What are we having for dinner?"

"I'm going to make the spaghetti I never got to make last time because we had that huge fight and you went home," Saint replies, glancing around the table. "If anything goes wrong this time, one of you please stop her from leaving."

"What could go wrong this time? Unless you have more baby mamas and secret children, I think we're good," I say, arching my brow.

"None that I know of," he replies, the men chuckling at his smart-ass answer.

"I'm going to kill you," I threaten, eyes narrowed to green slits. "This better be the best fucking pasta that has ever entered my mouth."

"It's pretty good," he says, standing up and winking at me. "You going to come help me in the kitchen?"

"I'll supervise," I agree, standing up and following him. "Do we have any wine?"

"Is he driving you to drink already?" Hammer calls out.

"Yes," I call back, and then all I can hear is laughter. Whether it's at me, or with me, I have no idea.

"Yeah, I'll get you a glass," Saint says. I sit back and watch him work the kitchen, first getting me wine, then starting to cook. "How was your day?"

"Good," I tell him, perking up at the thought. "We're doing anatomy right now and there's so much to remember, but it's interesting, so I don't mind it. I'm going to have to do some studying tonight."

"Oh, need someone to help you study?" he asks, turning around from the stove with a wooden spoon in his hand.

"Yeah, actually. I was thinking of asking Reece, this really cute guy from class," I reply, getting him back for his baby mama comment outside.

Now he's the one with narrowed eyes. "You're giving this Reece guy a death sentence if you decide to continue."

I sip my wine, pinky finger sticking out. "Now, now, Saint. Let's not get violent. Also, he's a martial arts expert."

I put my glass down just in time for Saint to grab me and lift me up. I wrap my legs around him and hold on to his neck.

"You just don't want to eat my spaghetti," he says to me, lip twitching. "That's what all this is about, isn't it? Or has the spaghetti left you traumatized after last time?"

"No, it hasn't left me with PTSD, don't worry." I smirk, kissing his nose. "I'm just feeling a little…"

"Sexually frustrated?" he offers, laughing out loud. "Is that why you're pushing me? Babe, if you want me, all you have to do is ask. Hell, all you have to do is look at me. I'm always wanting you and I will always be ready for you."

I put my hand over his mouth when I hear footsteps near us. If my dad heard that, I'm going to die a little inside.

It's Renny who sticks his face in the kitchen. "What the hell is going on in here? You're supposed to be cooking, Saint, not having your way with the prez's daughter in the middle of the day." He barks out a laugh before disappearing. "You have some balls, brother. Balls of fucking steel. I'd be pretending I was a virgin while Hammer is around."

Saint puts me down and I pick up my glass once more, resuming my position. When I down the rest of it, Saint murmurs something about needing some of the wine for the pasta.

Maybe he's right and I am sexually frustrated, but it's not like I'm going without. Saint and I have sex pretty much every night we spend together. He's created a monster. Or maybe I'm just hangry, which is also a possibility. When I glance over at him he's picking up a tea towel that fell on the floor, and I can't stop looking at his ass, his strong thighs...

Fuck, he's right.

I'm addicted to his D. This is going to be a problem.

Speaking of D... "Why do you guys call Wade *Dee*?"

Saint turns to me with brows furrowed. "How the hell do you know his name is Wade? I didn't even know that."

"I saw his credit card when he came into work once. Remember, I told you—his first date with Maryanne," I explain.

He nods. "Oh yeah, that's right. They call him Dee because he's the biggest dick."

"Biggest dick or he has the biggest dick?" I ask, dead serious. Why else would they call him that when his name is fucking Wade?

And guess who decides to walk in just as I say that?

All I can hear is the bastard's laughter, like a fucking hyena, absolutely losing his shit.

"What the fuck is so funny?" Temper asks as he comes to see what all the commotion is about.

Dee can't breathe at this point, so when he tries to tell Temper what I said, it just ends up in more fits of laughter.

"Sky is asking how Dee got his nickname," Saint says, scrubbing a hand down his face. He looks like he's torn between laughing and killing me. "And she's come to the scientific conclusion that he's either a huge dick or has a huge dick."

Pointing my finger in the air, I sophistically state, "I believe it's a valid conclusion. I mean, Saint got his name because he's a man whore, right? You guys were trying to be funny."

Saint always tried to maintain that he got his road name because he was a Saint compared to the others, but I learned long ago that it's because he always had a way with the ladies.

"I'm reformed," Saint adds in, finally admitting the truth.

"Temper got his because…well. He's apparently a psycho."

"And how did I get my name?" Dad asks as he joins us, amusement plainly written on his face.

Hammer?

Ew.

The only thing I can come up with is something I'd rather not think about.

Ever.

"I need more wine," I declare, looking for the bottle.

And this motherfucking conversation is over.

Chapter Twenty-Six

I can tell that something is wrong the second I step inside the clubhouse—the atmosphere so thick and tense, it's a struggle to breathe. There is a tension in the air that's just festering. Searching for Saint, I find him sitting outside at the table with the men.

All of the men, and all of them looking very serious.

After all the time during my childhood spent at the clubhouse, I know this isn't a time to intrude. I walk back inside and wait in his bedroom. I hope no one is in trouble with the police, and that no one is in danger. Did one of their deals go wrong? I know that they run several businesses, like Saint said, and not all of them are legal.

Things have been so lighthearted around here recently that it's easy to forget what they do to earn their money; they don't exactly have a nine to five. I don't really think about what each of these men I call my family are capable of. I just go by how they treat me, and that's all that I focus on. Maybe it's naïve, but it's how it needs to be.

I fall asleep with my book in my hands, and wake when Saint opens the door and comes in. "Sleeping beauty," he says, lying down next to me. "Sorry to keep you waiting."

"Is everything okay?" I ask, reaching for him. "Seemed pretty heated."

"Yeah, there's an issue, but we're going to sort it out, so don't worry. Unfortunately I'm going to have to go and do the rounds tonight with Temper, so I'm not going to be able to stay in and do all the things I want to do with you. Will you stay here, though? I want to come home to you in my bed," he asks, kissing me softly, which soon turns heated.

Lifting myself up, I lower my body onto his and strad-dle him. "Do you have to leave right now?"

Someone bangs on our door. "Saint! We're leaving!"

"I guess that's a yes," I whisper, leaning over to kiss him and then roll off.

"Well, you just made my night that much harder," he groans, glancing down at his cock.

I bury my smile into the pillow. "Great pun. I'll see you later tonight then."

He groans again, gets out of bed and comes around to my side, kissing my cheek. "Just wait until I get back, you little tease."

"Be safe."

"I will. Renny will be here if you need anything."

Another kiss, and then he's gone.

Not knowing what is happening or what we are deal-ing with is hell. I know I could push and get more out of him if I wanted to, but I'd rather him just tell me what he feels comfortable with. The MC is my family, but I'm not a member, and I know there's a difference. I trust them, and that they will handle any situations that arise.

While I study, Renny locks up the clubhouse and makes sure everything is closed. They should really amp up the security here. I know they only have security cameras and the big fence, which they usually just leave open because there's so many people coming in and out. I think they live by the "no one is stupid enough to come in here" law, but they should be smarter about it.

I fall asleep without Saint, and when I wake up in the morning he's not in bed, either.

Finding him in the gym, I watch as he punches the shit out of a boxing bag, shirtless. "You didn't sleep?" I ask when he stops to take a break.

"I did, but just for a couple hours," he explains, wiping his face with a towel. "You were knocked out so I didn't want to wake you, although trust me when I say I was tempted."

"You could have," I say. "I'll go and make us some breakfast."

I'm frying bacon, and the smell brings in Dad and Renny, so I end up making breakfast for everyone. "Bacon, eggs, toast, mushrooms and hash browns," I say, placing the plates full of food on the table for them to serve themselves.

"Thank you," Dad says, and I don't miss the bags under his eyes. "Looks like none of you got any sleep last night."

I know Saint said he had to do the runs with Temper, which means he was checking on their businesses or whatever, but there's obviously something going on because they all look exhausted and their morale seems kind of low. I open my mouth, but decide to close it and make some coffee instead. Coffee might perk them up a bit.

"Is there anything you guys want me to do before I head to class? I could drop off some lunch for everyone on my break," I offer, glancing around the table.

"We're okay, Sky," Saint assures me, standing behind me and massaging my shoulders. "You just worry about your class, and we can sort ourselves out. Are you here tonight or at Logan's?"

"Logan's," I tell him. "Tonight is family night with my brothers, so basically we're all going to eat, drink and talk shit and rip on each other until we call it a night."

I clean up and then head to class, but I can't shake off this bad feeling in my gut. Something is going on.

"So we actually have some news tonight," Logan announces, clicking a spoon on his bottle of beer. He has Smith and Axel on video chat, so I know this news must be big.

"You won the lottery?" Seth screams.

"You're visiting us here in Ireland!" Axel says enthusiastically.

"You're getting a dog," I add hopefully.

"You found out you were really adopted?" Brooks asks, garnering a smack in the back of the head from Seth.

Logan rolls his eyes at Brooks. "Sabrina is pregnant! You lot will finally have a niece or nephew."

"What?" I shout, jumping up and running to Logan to hug him. I know how long they have tried for a baby, and I'm so happy for it to finally happen for them.

"What about me? I'm the pregnant one," Sabrina teases, so I give her a hug too.

"Congratulations to you both. Just telling you now that Skylar is an amazing name, and I'm not against having another one in the family."

"One Skylar is enough, thanks!" Brooks calls out, eyebrows high on his smug face.

"Hopefully it's a girl because I'm tired of being out-numbered," I say, looking back at him. "And also sur-rounded by assholes."

"Are you sure? Because you have the same thing at the clubhouse," Brooks fires back, chuckling to himself. The rest of my brothers join in.

I throw daggers at Logan, the most mature one, but he just shrugs. "Oh, come on. That was funny."

We all speak to Smith and Axel, who are over the moon for Logan, and it's really nice to see their faces. Axel tells me that they'll be coming back soon and will try to stay in the city long enough for me to spend ac-tual time with them, which warms my heart.

The pizza Seth ordered us all arrives, and we sit in front of the TV and eat. It's the quietest it's been since we walked into the house.

"How's class been?" Seth asks me. He's the brother who has been the most interested in my education from the get-go, and when he found out I have decided to be-come a paramedic, he was so proud of me.

"Really good, I'm learning so many new things every day," I tell him, swallowing my mouthful of pepperoni. "It's both mentally stimulating and physical when we do the practical stuff, so it's really interesting."

"I'm glad you're studying again. You're such a smart girl, Skylar. You always have been," he continues, reach-ing over and touching my shoulder. Seth isn't very af-fectionate, so him actually touching me of his own free will is kind of a big thing. Usually it's me hugging him, and him awkwardly standing there and taking it.

"Thanks, Seth," I reply, beaming. "It feels good to be moving forward instead of being stuck in the same place and routine like I was in my last job. And the bar job I'm in now, I actually don't mind it, maybe because I know I won't be there forever."

It's going to be nice having some options for a change, and some sort of qualifications behind me, not to mention financial security. I don't want to have to live paycheck to paycheck for the rest of my life, and I also don't want to have to rely on Saint for anything. Logan told the rest of my brothers what happened with Mom, and I don't know if they're in contact with her or not, but I'm fine with it either way. They haven't asked me anything about Saint or Hammer, so it's not like anyone is trying to get information out of me to pass on to her. She's just like the elephant in the room, and no one wants to bring her up or discuss what happened so we're all just going to pretend she doesn't exist.

And I'm more than okay with that.

It's easier this way.

Chapter Twenty-Seven

"I have it all under control," I hear Dad say. I've shown up unannounced at the clubhouse, and with the loud talking they mustn't have heard me enter.

"They aren't going to stop—it's not safe for any of us right now. Either we take him down, or we're sitting ducks," Temper chimes in.

Instead of making myself known, I step back and listen to their conversation. They will never tell me what's going on, and although I feel bad, I really want to be included this time.

"I know," Hammer growls, a large bang, one that sounds like him slamming his fist on the table, makes me jump. "I fucking know, all right? We need to make a plan, and we need one now. It feels like five years ago all over again. When will this end, though? His brother died, and he wants revenge. But if we take him out, then what? Is there another fucking brother we have to look out for?"

"Nope, just the two of them," I hear Saint add in. "It's not safe right now, and yeah, we need a plan. I don't want Sky in any kind of danger."

"And you think I do?" Hammer fires back, tone lethal. "No one we care about is going to get hurt. We just need to find this guy, and... Fuck. Why did he have to get out of prison? I know we can handle him. The question is, can we handle him without any of us doing time?"

Silence for a few seconds.

I step back a little then walk to Saint's room instead, my head buzzing with everything I just overheard.

Revenge?

Sitting ducks?

Could they be talking about the man Mom offered to hand me over to? It makes sense, because that man did end up in prison. The past has come back to haunt us all.

This time I'm older, and there's no one to throw me under the bus like last time. But I still have no idea how I can help. I don't want anything to happen to any of the men, and I don't know what I'd do if it did.

Saint comes in about thirty minutes later and I pretend to be fast asleep.

"I didn't even hear you come in," he whispers as he jumps in bed with me.

Snuggling up to him instantly, I struggle between ignoring everything I just heard and acting normal or confronting him. I decide on the latter. "I heard what you guys were talking about."

Saint sighs and lifts my face up to look him in the eye. "We will handle it, all right? You don't need to worry, but I just want you to be a little more vigilant than usual. Don't trust anyone you don't know and just be extra street smart in all situations."

"What's happening exactly, Saint? No more bullshit. This affects me too," I say to him, frowning. "Is this the same guy that was after Hammer when I left? The one Mom wanted to use me as a bartering tool with?"

"Yeah, that's him. Killer. He's been in prison all of

these years, but he's finally been let out and apparently hasn't let go of his vendetta. His brother died, so I guess it's understandable," he says, words turning to mumbles.

"His brother was hit," Saint says, wincing. "And he fell back and knocked his head and died. It was a big group brawl, so we don't even know who hit who, but it was us they were fighting, so Killer decided to take it out on our president and swore Hammer would pay for him losing his little brother."

"But then he got locked up," I whisper, finally understanding the situation. "So what are you guys going to do? We all have to protect Hammer."

"Yeah, basically we're all going to be on guard," Saint says, kissing my forehead. "He might want Hammer, but none of us are safe until the threat is stabilized. If Killer sees his opportunity, he's going to take it."

"What did he go to prison for?" I ask, trying to formulate a plan. I might not be able to fight or anything like that, but I'm smart, and I'm good at problem solving.

"Assault. But that was his second offense, so he didn't get a lenient sentence like I did."

"Okay, so he's on probation now, I'm assuming, which means he can't step out of line. What if we try to get him locked up again? I don't want any of the Knights having to go to prison because of this guy."

Or getting hurt, or worse. I don't want any of them having to end someone's life to protect my dad's. I don't want anything to happen to my dad, either. It's hard to win in this situation without someone being sacrificed.

"And what about my brothers, are they all safe?" If something happened to any of them, I wouldn't be able to live with myself.

"Your brothers will be fine, but we will give them

a heads-up just to be safe. If it gets bad we will have a shutdown, where anyone we love can come here and be safe. Trust me, we don't want that either, but if it's us or them, it's going to be them," he states, a hard look in his pretty blue eyes. "I don't want you to worry about anything other than keeping yourself safe. If it gets to a critical point, we're going to go into lockdown, and you will be escorted to classes or work, or wherever. It's better to be safe than sorry, all right?"

I nod. "All right." I love my freedom, but I'm not stupid. These men aren't messing around and I'm going to be careful.

"Good girl," he whispers, sighing. "I'm sorry you have to deal with all this."

"Don't worry about me," I tell him. "I'm just worried about all of you. I can't lose you, Saint."

"You won't," he replies, sounding confident. He even manages to flash me a cheeky grin. "When I have you in my bed, there's no way I'm not going to return to it."

"Be serious."

"I am being serious," he says, rolling me over and holding my wrists down against the mattress. "I love you."

"And I love you."

The sooner this whole situation comes to an end, the better.

Killer needs to go back behind bars where he belongs.

"Tory, what are you doing?" I ask the energetic toddler as she runs around the clubhouse, leaving a spiral of disaster everywhere she goes. I don't know how moms do it, because this looking after a small person thing is no joke, and I'm watching Tory only while Saint's out to get us some lunch and run some errands.

"Don't you like the new toys I bought you?" I ask, eying the discarded pile. Instead she seems to enjoy playing with the box one of the dolls came in.

"I like," she says, nodding, but continues to drag the box around. I follow her into the kitchen and watch as she tries to open up the cupboard.

"Are you hungry?"

She looks at me with those blue eyes and nods again. "Yes."

"Okay," I say opening the fridge. "How about some yogurt?"

She cheers, so I'm guessing that's a yes.

I sit her at the table with a spoon and watch her shovel the yogurt into her mouth. She really is a cute little kid. Her mom did the DNA test, so we're just waiting on the results now, but I think it's obvious that Saint is her dad. I don't know why she said otherwise—maybe she just wanted to hurt him and get more leverage over him.

"Yum," Tory mumbles, placing the cup down and looking up at me. "More?"

"More, please?" I suggest to her.

"More pweese."

Grinning, I grab her another tub and some blueberries. "Your dad better hurry up with the food or you're going to be full by the time he gets here."

I hear the rumble of his motorcycle just as those words leave my mouth. "Oh, he's here. Can you hear the sound of his bike?"

Tory nods, eyes going wide. "Bike loud."

"It is pretty loud, isn't it?" I agree.

Saint comes in with bags of food, smiling when he sees both of us sitting there. "Sorry it took so long."

"That's okay. Your little girl got hungry, though, so she had some snacks," I tell him.

He comes over to me and kisses the top of my head. "Why do you do that?"

"Why do I do what?" I ask him, lifting my head back to look up at him.

"You always say 'your little girl' or 'your daughter,' emphasizing the 'your.' I'm going to marry you one day, Skylar, which means she's yours too. Just because you didn't give birth to her doesn't mean she's not your family. You should know more than anyone that blood doesn't always mean the most."

"I didn't even realize I was doing that," I admit, and never would I have thought my wording would upset him. I don't see Tory as mine in any way—at least I don't consider myself her second mother or anything like that—but I do care about her and would do anything for her. So I think that has to count for something. Saint is right, of course. Blood isn't everything—loyalty is.

"You're a part of this family," he says, kissing me again, and then unloading the food. I know he's making sure I feel included and I appreciate it, but he doesn't need to. I've accepted the situation as it is, and I'm going to make the best of it.

"I know, Saint. And thank you for making me feel that way."

We have lunch, and then I head off to work, leaving Saint to have some alone time with his daughter. Carol seems to be slowly letting him have her more, and I wonder if it's because the results are going to arrive within the next few weeks and we're all going to know the truth about Tory's paternity. Or maybe she's just in a good mood with all the extra money she's been getting.

Either way, we get to see Tory, so that's all that matters.

Chapter Twenty-Eight

As I'm leaving class, the last person in the world that I want to see is standing next to my car. After having such a good morning—spending some much needed alone time with Saint and then a great class where I got high marks on a test—I feel like my day is about to be ruined.

"What are you doing here, Mom?" I ask, searching for my keys in my handbag. "You have no daughter, remember? So why don't you go and visit one of your sons? You have plenty of them."

I don't know how she knew I'm doing this program or what time I'd be here, but I hate that she does. She's obviously still keeping tabs on me, which annoys me to no end.

"I just want to talk," she says, pursing her lips. "Can you give me that, at least? I want to apologize. I know I'm not a perfect mother and that I've messed up, but I want a chance to apologize and explain some things to you. This is all my fault, and it's time that I told you who your real father is. Do you have time for a coffee? I'll explain everything from start to finish."

"I thought you didn't know who my father was," I remind her, frowning. She's dangling the bait right in front of my face, but it's the one thing that I've always wanted to know. "Was that a lie too?"

I don't know how much more of this I can take. The back and forth, it's so exhausting. I wouldn't be surprised if she knew this whole time who my biological father is and just didn't tell me. Not that it would matter. Hammer is my father.

"I have my reasons, and when I explain, you'll understand everything," she promises.

"Okay, I guess we can have a coffee," I decide, willing to hear what she has to say. "There's a place down the road. We can walk there or drive."

"Let's drive. I'll walk back once we're done," she suggests.

"Okay," I say, opening the car door. She gets in, and we buckle up and leave.

"I really am sorry, Skylar. I took you out of that world for a purpose, and when I found out you had gone back there, I just lost it," she says, sniffling a little. "And I'm sorry about the money. I still have some of it and I will give it to you. I'm sorry about everything. I've been a terrible mother. I hope you can forgive me."

She got dumped—she didn't choose to leave and save me like she is now claiming—but I don't bring that up to her. You can't argue with crazy, and she's the queen of talking shit, so she's going to have an answer for everything.

After parking my car in the coffee shop lot, I turn to her about to ask her if she really knows who my dad is.

Instead, I'm greeted with a sharp knock to my head, and all goes black.

When I wake up, my head is pounding. I don't think it has ever hurt so much in my life. Rubbing the back of it gently, I force my eyes open and glance around at my surroundings. I'm in a room, which is bare except for a mattress on the floor. The windows have been barred with big pieces of wood, blocking any light from getting in.

A sick feeling in my stomach, I sit up and remember how I got here—because I trusted my mother when she said she wanted a fucking coffee and an adult chat about everything that has happened. I'm here because I wanted some closure, and in return, I get knocked out and kidnapped by the woman who gave birth to me. This takes family drama to a whole new level.

Moving to the locked door, I bang on it loudly. "Mom! Let me out!" I yell, banging harder.

What the hell is she going to do with me? I have no idea what she has planned, but I know it can't be good. The fact she has crossed this line means she has clearly lost her mind—I need to never underestimate her again.

Wherever she's decided to put me, she obviously thought about this. I try to pull the wooden planks off the window, but they don't budge. There's nothing I can use as a weapon, and no way I can break out of here except through the door.

I was going straight home after class and not to the clubhouse, so the MC isn't even expecting me, and I don't even know if Logan is home to realize that I'm missing.

Basically, I'm fucked.

I scream until my voice is broken, then fall back onto the mattress in a pile, not sure what the hell I'm meant to do or how I'm going to get out of this. Why didn't I just drive off and leave her there? I thought I was fine and had accepted my situation with her. But no, I'm still a little girl who needed her mother to love her, who wanted to know the truth behind the father who I've never known. Stupid idiot that I am.

Hand on my forehead, I curse myself for thinking there was even an ounce of good in her. Getting back up, I place my ear against the door and listen for any sounds or movement but hear nothing. Is she out there? Deciding all I can do is play the waiting game and see what she has in store for me, I sit back on the bed and pray that Logan has called Saint or Hammer.

I don't know how much time passes, an hour maybe, but the door finally opens, and it's not my mother. A man stands there, one I've never seen before. A very large man. He's dressed in black and worn leather, and looks like his personal hygiene isn't a high priority with him.

He grins evilly when he sees me, revealing teeth too big for his mouth, surrounded by a beard that needs a good wash. "Skylar O'Connor," he says, cracking his knuckles.

"Who are you?" I ask, back literally against the wall. "Where's my mother? And what do you want with me?" I can't believe that once again, my own mother has thrown me under the bus. At this stage, I don't know why I'm so surprised, but the hurt and betrayal is still there, ripe as ever. I never should have given her a second of my time, or thought that she was human and wanted to apologize.

I've fucked up, big time. My stupid bleeding heart that wanted her mother to love her. Idiot.

"You, my girl, are going to be used as bait to bring Hammer here," he tells me, booming with laughter.

"Killer?" I guess, starting to panic.

"Oh, you've heard of me then? Good. You're about to

find out how I got my road name," he declares, stepping closer to me. "You're a pretty little thing, aren't you?"

Fucking creep. "Don't fucking touch me," I warn him, placing my hands in front of me. "Besides, aren't I a little old for you?"

He laughs harder. He clearly belongs in a mental ward and instead he's been let out of prison to ruin other people's lives. "I like you, Skylar." He leans forward and adds, "And that's probably not going to end well for you."

Great.

He moves back to the door, and I relax a little, my shoulders slouching. Movement from behind him brings none other than my mother into view.

"Mom, don't leave me here!" I call out, pleading with my eyes. "I am your only daughter—how can you do this to me?"

"You'll be fine," she replies with a shrug. "It's just Hammer we want, Skylar. And after we have him, we will let you go. No harm will come to you."

She acts like that makes all of this okay, that just because I will be able to walk out of here, it's no big deal. She's batshit crazy.

"How can you do this to him?" I ask her, feeling tears threaten. "He raised me! You loved him more than your own kids at one point—how can you do this to us?"

"Don't bother begging, little one," Killer says to me, his beady, dead eyes looking right into mine. "My brother died, and now someone has to pay. A tooth for a tooth. If not Hammer, then who? Would you rather someone else take his place?"

I feel bad, but my mother does come to mind.

"Killer, give it a rest." She pushes him aside and steps toward me. I instinctively take a step back. "I told you I was going to tell you who your father was," Mom says, looking at me unflinchingly in the eye. "I never wanted you to find out the truth, but I agree. It's time you knew the whole truth.

"When I met Kieran—that's your father—I was a single mother with five boys at home. I fell for him, and I fell for him hard. When you were born, you were the apple of his eye. He looked at you like you hung the moon."

I want to smile at the thought that my biological father, whoever he is, loved me. Truly loved me, but I bury those feelings for another time.

"I hated that he loved you so much. Loved you more than me and my boys. He didn't want anything to do with your brothers. I don't even think they remember him." She sneers. "I couldn't let him ignore my sons and I couldn't let him put you before me. So I took you away from him. I left and changed my name, and met Hammer a few months later. And Hammer loved *me*. Sure, he loved you too, but he loved me in a way Kieran didn't.

"When you were sixteen, Kieran found me. And he was furious that I had kept you from him for years. I knew he'd come after you and he'd make me pay for what I did."

"Mom, this is a great story, but I have no idea what that has to do with the fact that you basically kidnapped me." I glare at her.

"He was my brother," Killer says. I look at him in confusion. "Kieran was my brother."

And just like that all the pieces fit into place. The reason why the Knights of Fury started catching heat from Killer and his MC. The reason why my mother never told me, or Hammer, who my biological father was.

For just a moment, Killer looks almost human as emotions cross his face. "Kieran was the best part of me. He hated your mother for what she did, but he loved you." He stares at me. "You look like our mother, actually." He actually sort of smiles.

My own mother rolls her eyes. "The Knights killed Kieran, Skylar. They killed your father. When I offered you up to Killer, I knew he wouldn't hurt you, because you are his blood."

"You have got to be kidding me. You want me to think that you were doing me a favor? You're nothing but a selfish, sad woman…"

She slaps me across the face. "Listen to me. If Killer had you, a piece of his brother, they'd leave the Knights alone and I'd be able to stay with Hammer. I loved him and—"

"And you offered up your daughter in exchange for your own happiness."

She opens her mouth to speak but then closes it.

"So what do you want now? Why are you working with him? Why after all this time?" I point over to Killer.

"I found her," Killer simply says. "I spent years in prison planning what I would do when I got out. Every plan I had came down to finding your mother. She is the reason why my brother is dead. She is the reason my brother missed out on sixteen years with his daughter. But then she changed my mind, and offered me something better."

I look at her. Shocked that she once again offered up her own daughter to save herself. "And you told him what? That I'd go with him?"

"No, I told him I'd get him Hammer. On a silver platter. But he promised he'd let you live your life, without any interference. See, I'm not as evil as you paint me out to be, Skylar. I was thinking of you."

I look to Killer. "Is this true?"

If it is, the monster standing before me is none other than my uncle.

"It's true," he admits. "It's the only reason you aren't bleeding out on the floor right now. That and because of my brother." He looks at Mom and points to his watch. "You have a few hours or else our arrangement will have to change." He turns to leave and slams the door closed.

"Mom, what the fuck is wrong with you? What are you doing?"

"I'm doing what mothers do. I'm protecting you," and with that she turns and leaves.

I'm left alone once more with all these new revelations. I can never tell if my mom is lying or not, but I feel like she might have actually been telling the truth. It's such a twisted end to the story that is my life, my biological father dead by the hands of the men who actually raised me and cared for me. I try to feel sad for him, but it's hard to grieve a man you never met. The worst part of this whole thing is that Kieran seemed like a decent guy. It's my mother who was the problem. She is to blame for all of this. Her and Killer.

Pushing Kieran out of my mind, I concentrate on the task at hand: getting out of here and not letting any of the Knights fall into the trap that my mother has set.

I need to trust in the Knights right now, and know that they're going to come up with a plan and save me. A plan that will get us *all* out of here safely. And alive.

And if not?

I'm going to save my damn self somehow.

When Killer opens the door and leaves some water and a sandwich on the floor, I feel like I'm in prison. Both the food and the company are shit.

"I need to pee," I tell him, because even prison has a toilet in their cell.

His jaw tenses, but if I'm such an inconvenience, then he shouldn't have kidnapped me in the first place. I regret my request as soon as he comes closer, grabs me by the arm and hauls me up. "Try anything, and trust me when I say you're going to regret it."

Swallowing hard, I let him drag me outside the bedroom, revealing an old, messy, and what looks to be abandoned house. The type of house that should have been knocked down years ago, and now is being used for nefarious under-the-radar purposes.

"Nice place you have here," I say, unable to keep my mouth shut.

I get a grunt in return.

When I see the bathroom, my jaw drops open. "This is worse than prison."

"Yeah," Killer agrees, clicking his tongue. "It's dirtier, isn't it? Enjoy, princess."

He throws me in and slams the door shut. I place toilet paper on the seat before sitting down, then wash up after I finish my business. I guess I should be grateful there is toilet paper and soap.

I check the bathroom for anything I could use to defend myself. It doesn't even have a mirror, or I could have tried to smash off a piece of it, like I once saw in a movie. Instead, I'm left with a toothbrush. I know professionals would somehow turn that into a shank, but I'm not on that level, so I don't bother.

"Fuck," I whisper, hands clenching to fists.

Think, Skylar, think.

The bang on the door makes me jump. "Hurry up!"

he yells in his booming voice, banging once more. "Your bladder can't be that big."

Opening the door, I step outside, given up on the toothbrush, only to be grabbed by the neck and hauled back toward the room.

Starting to panic, I realize this might be my only time to escape, but how the hell am I supposed to fight off this huge-ass man? He's easily three times my size, built like a tree house and as muscley as any man who is trying to compensate for his small penis. Still, if I don't try now, I'm going to be put back into that room and will be just sitting there waiting on other people to save me.

Fuck it.

I wait until we are just before the room, and glance down the hallway which must lead to either a front or back door—hopefully the front—and then spin around quickly and kick my leg up as hard as I possibly can, hitting him right in the nuts.

He might be a fucking beast but even that takes him down, and he falls to his knees while I run down the hallway and out the door, only to run into two men. Men I've seen before. They are the ones I saw at my workplace, Dumb and Dumber, watching me and giving me the creeps.

I try to escape them by running, but quickly fail, one man grabbing me and throwing me over his shoulder.

"And where the hell do you think you're going?" Dumber rumbles, slapping me hard on the butt. "We aren't done with you yet."

I scream, I kick, I hit. I do everything I can to make it harder for them to drag me back inside, but between the two of them, they manage to do just that, and I'm thrown back into the room, landing on my back, which fucking hurts.

"Try that again, and we won't be so nice," Dumber threatens, slamming the door shut. Thankfully, Killer doesn't come back in, but I hear his booming voice and he sounds extremely unhappy with me.

Shit.

Things are not looking good.

"Saint," I whisper, lip trembling.

Where are you?

Chapter Twenty-Nine

I get hungry, so I eat the damn food Killer left me, hating that I couldn't hold out for any longer. But with nothing to do except plan different scenarios in my head and how I would react in each one, I'm bored and nervous and waiting for the pin to drop.

What feels like an eternity later, the door opens and Killer stands there, a smug smirk on his gruesome face. "Today is your lucky day," he says, resting on the doorframe, his leather cut pressed against the powdered walls. "You get to go home."

"What happened?" I ask, standing. He looks way too happy to have lost in any way, and I'm almost too scared to find out what has happened.

He stays silent, so I yell, "Tell me!" If something has happened to Saint, or to Hammer, I don't have anything else to lose.

Killer closes the door, laughing. I call out, demanding answers, suddenly feeling bold and strong. I need to know if the men are okay.

When it comes to saving myself, I might have failed, but when it comes to saving someone that I love…

I'll never stop fighting.

When the door opens again, it's not Killer's face I see, or even my mother's.

It's Hammer's.

Relief fills me, but when I don't see Saint with him, confusion sets in. Is Saint okay?

Running to his arms, I jump against his chest and hold on tighter than I ever have before. "What the hell is going on?" I ask him. "How did you get in here? Where's Saint?"

I imagine the whole MC out in front, Killer and his henchmen no match for the Knights of Fury.

No one is.

"Saint is fine," he assures me, rubbing my back soothingly. "Everyone is fine, you don't need to worry, but I need you to listen to me, okay?"

I nod.

"I love you," he says. "You're the daughter I always wanted. I'm so proud of the woman you've become, and…yeah, I love you, Skylar. I've always loved you, and I want you to remember that."

He then whispers numbers into my ear—a code maybe? "Six, one, seven, three."

"Why are you telling me that?" I ask, confused.

"Just remember it."

So I memorize it: six, one, seven, three.

"I love you too, Hammer," I reply, holding on to him even tighter. "But we can tell each other this when we both get out and are safe back at the clubhouse."

He smiles sadly, and then slowly he slides his phone into the front pocket of my jeans, which I quickly cover with my T-shirt.

And then Killer appears behind him, and Hammer steps aside. Killer grabs my arm and starts pulling me toward the door, but I fight against him.

"No! Hammer! I want to stay with you, I'm not leaving you here!" I scream out.

Dumb and Dumber stand on each side of him. He could take them both, I know it. But all three? Probably not.

He'd put up a mean fight, though.

I realize he's not going to fight back until I'm safely outside, or maybe with the deal he's made he's not going to fight back at all. I don't want to think that he has given up, I don't want him to be a martyr, I want him to come home to me.

As I continue to fight Killer off, he grabs me by the neck and starts to squeeze, obviously tired of my shit.

"We had a deal," Hammer calls out, tone furious. "She is to be left unharmed!"

Killer loosens his hold, muttering a curse. "Can't wait to be rid of you, bitch."

The feeling is motherfucking mutual. "Fuck you. You're going to regret this, especially if anything happens to Hammer."

The last thing I see before stepping outside is Hammer mouthing my name.

It hits me then, that no, he's not going to fight back.

He's sacrificing himself for me. *We had a deal*, he said.

He put me before anything. Before the club and even himself. He put me first.

There's a car already waiting for me, with the door open, and a man dressed in all black stands next to it.

"You can't blame him for your brother's death, you piece of—"

Suddenly, something is pressed against my nose and my sight goes blurry, and then everything turns to oblivion.

* * *

When I wake up again, I have sand on my mouth, and I'm lying on the side of the road on my stomach in shrub. Sitting up and wiping my face, I stand up and eye the road, realizing that they have dropped me off not too far from the clubhouse. I have no idea how long I've been here, or how much time has passed. Remembering what happened, and Hammer, I force myself to run the full way back. I can only hope I'm not too late.

"Saint!" I yell out as soon as I reach the front. "Saint!"

The gate, which is usually unlocked, isn't budging. I try yelling out a little longer, but when there is no sign of anyone, I glance around, trying to think of what else to do next.

My mouth is dry, and I don't know how much time has passed or how long I was lying on the side of the fucking road. My phone was in my car, and the clubhouse doesn't have a land line anyway, so I don't know what the hell I'm supposed to be doing right now.

Running across the vacant blocks of land next to the clubhouse, I keep running until I come to our closest neighbor. I need a phone. Banging on the door, I realize I must look awful, and I hope they don't slam the door in my face and call the cops.

The door opens, and a woman stands there, taking me in through the screen door. She opens it too, eyes roaming over me. "Are you okay?"

"I'm Skylar, I'm from next door and I was wondering if I could use your phone. It's kind of an emergency," I rush out, bouncing on my feet in impatience.

"Next door as in the clubhouse?" she asks, frowning. "Yes, of course you can use my phone. Come on in."

I follow her inside as she grabs her phone from a wooden coffee table and hands it to me. "Thank you,"

I say to her, dialing Saint's number, which thank God I memorized, and putting it against my ear.

"Hello?" Saint asks, and I can hear some sort of commotion in the background.

"Saint?"

"Skylar? Where are you? We've been looking everywhere!" he says, tone panicked and laced with desperation.

"I'm next door to the clubhouse," I tell him. "At that woman's house—you know, the one Renny thinks is hot."

"Fuck, stay there. I love you," he says, hanging up the line on me.

"Thank you so much," I say to her, handing her phone back.

"No problem. I'm Isabella," she says, arching her brow. "And whoever Renny is, tell him I'm flattered."

I'd laugh in any other situation.

Isabella makes me a cup of coffee and sits with me out front on her swing until I hear the familiar rumble of motorcycles.

"He's here," I say, standing up and giving her the mug back. "Thank you so much. I owe you a beer or something. You're a lifesaver."

"No problem," she replies, standing up with me. "I hope everything is okay."

"Me, too," I say, waving to her and running toward Saint's bike. Temper and Renny are with him, and I have so many questions, but all I do is jump on his bike and ride off with him, squeezing him from behind in relief. Even if all we are doing is riding back to the clubhouse, being near him is what I need right now.

Saint is okay, and I'm back where I belong.

Now we just need to go back for Hammer.

Chapter Thirty

Saint stops at the clubhouse, and I get off his bike and hold on to him.

"Are you okay?" he asks, lifting me in the air. "I've never been so scared in my life, Skylar."

"I'm fine, and I wasn't hurt. Where is Hammer?" I ask. "He saved me and then stayed back, and I need to know if he's okay. Did he get out?"

Saint looks away, swallowing hard. "He left here without us. We don't know where he went—only he knew the address. We showed up at Killer's clubhouse, broke inside and raised hell, asking where our prez was, but he wasn't there. Killer was smart; no one there knew his location. No one."

I realize that while I know what the abandoned house looks like I don't know how to get there, either. I was out both times, going to and from the house, and now I know that was done on purpose, not just because I was carrying on and not making shit easy for them.

"Fuck!" I yell, stamping my foot. "It's an old abandoned house."

Temper and Renny come and stand around me. "What else can you tell us?" Temper asks.

"Mom was there, Killer, and two men. I've seen those two men before—they came into my work."

And then I remember something.

Lifting up my T-shirt, I pull a phone out of my pocket. "I'm such an idiot, I had this the whole time. Hammer gave it to me."

And only I know the pin. I type it in.

Temper holds out his hand. "Fuck, he knew this would be the only way we could track him. He turned his GPS tracking off." He goes through the call list. "This has to be Killer's number. We can try to track it down. Dee knows how to do all of that shit; I'll get him on the line. Rest of you get ready, we're going to go find him."

Saint turns to me, resting his arms on my shoulders. "I'm going to drop you at your brother's. It's not safe being here alone."

"No, I want to come. I can tell you if you're at the right place or not, I know what it looks like from the front," I say, watching Saint shake his head. "I'm coming. He's my dad, and he's only there because he saved me. I'm coming."

"No, you're not," Saint growls, fingers tightening on me. "I only just found you safe—you aren't going back there. It's too dangerous."

"It's dangerous for everyone, and you're all still going. Saint, if something happens to you and Hammer, I have nothing left. I want to be there. I know I can't do much, but you can't expect me to sit at home twiddling my fucking thumbs not knowing if any of you are dead or alive," I say, standing my ground.

"She's right. We need her to ID the building," Renny says to Saint, slapping him on the shoulder. "We'll all be there, brother. And she's a Knight too—you can't expect her to sit on the sidelines."

"You have no idea, Renny," Saint snarls back to him, stepping away from his touch. "When you find your old lady, you will, but right now you have no idea, and you need to stay out of this. Skylar is not coming, and that is that."

"Then I guess I'll ride on the back of Renny's bike," I say, walking toward it.

Saint grabs my by the waist and pulls my back against his chest. "I can't lose you, Skylar, and I almost did today. I won't..." He trails off, sucking in air. "Don't do this, please."

I hate seeing him like this, and I know that it's because he's scared something is going to happen to me and because he loves me, but I'm not backing down from this.

"I can't lose you either, Saint. Do you think I like you riding off and potentially never coming back? It goes both ways. Instead of fighting me, why don't you take me with you? We can protect each other," I say, turning to face him and looking him in the eye. "I'll try not to be a liability."

Temper runs out of the clubhouse, sliding a gun into his jeans. "Let's go. I've got an address. Dee and the other men are going to meet us there, and a few of them are bringing cars instead of bikes, so we can bring Hammer home."

Bring Hammer home.

I've never wanted anything more in my life.

Saint kisses me, deeply and hungrily, and then hands me a helmet. I put it on without any hesitation and get on the back of his bike. The engines start, like a chorus, and determination fuels me. I'm scared, terrified even, but I'm not going home without my dad.

We ride for about twenty minutes and then come to a stop in front of a house.

The house.

I look at Temper and nod. Dee found it.

"Shouldn't we have parked down the road and walked or something?" I ask Saint as we get off the motorcycle.

Saint passes me a handgun. "No time for being subtle. We're going in there and shooting, and asking questions later." He glances up and down at me. "Dee is here in his car. Go in there and wait with him."

"Okay." I nod, kissing Saint. "I love you."

"I love you too."

I run toward Dee's BMW and jump in the front seat. He parks across the road, keeping the engine on, ready to make a quick exit. Looking down at the gun in my hand, I turn to him. "What if they need more backup?"

"Five men went in," he says, lifting his own gun up and placing it out the window. "And I'm the sniper. So we're good. This isn't all done at random, Sky. We've planned this in case some shit went down. Every member knows what they're supposed to be doing and where they're supposed to be. You don't need to worry—this isn't our first rodeo."

"Interesting," I whisper, staring at the now open door of the house where they all entered. "And what is Saint's job?"

"Protect Temper, and to shoot first and ask questions later," Dee admits, eyes through the scope of the gun. "Temper protects Hammer. There's a hierarchy, and we always have someone watching out for us, like little brothers looking out for the big brothers."

We hear shots firing, and I find myself on the edge of my seat, praying that the men aren't hurt.

"Please let them be okay," I whisper, my fingernails digging into my palms.

Minutes later, I see them all coming out, and Temper and Saint are carrying Hammer in their arms. He's covered in blood and looks like he's taken a few too many hits to the face, but he's alive, and that's all that matters.

They put him in the back of the car and slam the door shut, telling Dee to take us to a hospital. I sit next to him, covering him with Dee's jacket, which I find in the back seat. "We have to go to the hospital!"

"I'll follow you," Saint tells me, running back to his bike.

Hammer reaches over and strokes my face. "My beautiful girl, what are you doing here?"

"Came to save you," I tell him. "From the car, though, because my SWAT skills are seriously lacking."

He laughs, then winces and coughs. "Don't make me laugh, Sky. It hurts."

Bracing myself, I lift up the jacket and see the gunshot wound. Holding the jacket on it to stop the bleeding, I look him in the eye, scared for him, but quickly turn my expression blank, not wanting him to see that in me.

"For once in my life, I've got you, Dad. It's always been the other way around," I say to him, smiling sadly.

"No it hasn't," he replies, closing his eyes. "I never should have let Georgia take you away from me. It doesn't matter that she was your mother, I always loved you more, and I shouldn't have ever let you leave your family."

"It doesn't matter now. I'm here, and that's all that matters," I tell him, kissing his cheek.

He nods, but I can see that he's slowly spacing out and might lose consciousness soon. "How far away are we?" I ask Dee, keeping the pressure on the wound.

"Five minutes," he replies.

"We're almost there," I tell Hammer, trying to keep him awake. "Don't worry, okay? We're almost there."

"What's the code I told you, Skylar?" he asks me.

"Six, one, seven, three," I whisper, scanning his eyes as he opens them and looks at me. "Why? What is it for?"

"Just remember it, okay? It's important."

I'm curious, but now is not the time to worry about small details like this one.

"I won't forget," I promise him. "But you can remind me what it is after we leave the hospital, okay? Trust me, I'll have plenty of questions about what it means."

"You were never one to shy away from questions," he mutters, but his lip twitches, like it's something he likes about me.

"Speaking of questions, what happened to Killer?" I ask Hammer.

"Let's just say he needs to change his road name," he replies, panting, his face etched in pain. He takes a deep breath before continuing to speak. "You don't have to worry about him, or any of them anymore, Skylar. I can rest easy now. You'll be safe, and the MC will always look after you. You always have a home there, for life, all right?"

My heart breaks with each word he utters, and fear starts to take over me.

"There will be no resting easy for you just yet. You're speaking like you're not going to be here when that's not the case, Dad. We're almost at the hospital, aren't we, Dee? Look, I can see it in the distance. We're all going to be fine, including you, and tomorrow you're going to yell at me about bringing a gun and pretending I'm some fucking heroine when in reality I have no idea what I'm doing, and I probably almost died a few times today, and…"

I stop my rant and look at Dad, cupping his cheek tenderly, my fingers trembling.

No.

"Dad?" I whisper, shaking him gently. "Dee, he passed out. Dad?" I repeat. "Wake up, you need to wake up."

"Fuck. We're here. Hide the weapons, Skylar, I'm going to run in and get a doctor," he says, parking the car, then handing me his rifle and bolting inside. I hide the guns under the seat and keep talking to Dad, hoping he can hear me.

"You know I was curious about my biological father, but I never cared about him, because I had you. If I wasn't curious about what Mom had to say, maybe we wouldn't be here right now. I don't know why I cared. This is my fault," I whisper, tears streaming down my face, my voice quivering. "I love you, Dad. More than anything."

Dee appears with two nurses and a stretcher. I get out of the car and watch as they place him on the stretcher, and rush him inside.

"I'll go wait with him," I say to Dee.

"I'll make sure everyone else is okay and meet you back here," he tells me, giving me a hug and a kiss on my temple before he leaves.

After I rush into the hospital, the nurse tells me to sit down in the waiting room and they will let me know when I can go in to see him. So I sit there, staring at nothing, just wondering how the fuck my life came to this moment right here. Glancing down at the blood on my hands, I realize I must look how I feel.

This year has been a whirlwind, and so many things have happened, but all I want to do is walk through those clubhouse doors and annoy the men, and see what they're up to. I want to cook for them, and I want to laugh with them, and have a beer with them. Everything I took for granted, I want it back. I want Hammer to be okay.

"I'll never ask for anything else," I whisper. "Just please let him be okay. Please. Don't take away the only parent that I have left."

I've never prayed as much as I have today.

And maybe that's why I didn't get what I wanted.

Chapter Thirty-One

The doctor comes straight over to me and by the look on his face, I can tell that he doesn't have good news.

"Are you with Xavier Dixon?" he asks, looking at my blood-covered hands. I should've gone to the bathroom to clean up, but I couldn't move.

It takes me a moment to respond. I'm not used to people using Hammer's real name. "Yes, I'm his daughter."

Words have never been more true. I don't care what Mom said about Killer's brother—Hammer is and always will be my dad.

"I'm sorry. We tried as best we could, but his injuries were too severe," he says, and the second those words leave his mouth, my body freezes. I feel cold throughout my body. The tears have stopped and I'm just frozen.

"We tried to save him," the doctor continues. "He was shot through the stomach and in the lung, and he lost so much blood…" He glances away from me, like he can't bear to continue talking and looking at me at the same time. "He's gone. I'm sorry."

My head spins. There's a sudden loud noise in my ears as what he's saying hits me, like I'm trying to block the words out. Like that can save me right now.

Shaking my head, I say, "Can I see him?" I won't

believe that he's gone until I see it with my own eyes. He can't be gone.

The doctor nods and a nurse leads me to a room. Hammer lies there on the bed, blood still covering him. Stepping closer, I take his large hand in mine and hold it. I think I'm in shock, because I don't say anything, I just stand here, numb.

He honored his promise to me. He was the only person who loved me enough to put me first. He was the only loving parent I ever had. And now he's gone…

He's not gone, he can't be. He's right here in front of me. I refuse to accept this.

I don't know how long I stand here like this, but then I'm surrounded by those I love. Saint's arms are around me, and Temper's burning anger and utter devastation. Renny's warmth and Dee's silent strength. I truly thought we were going to get out of this unscathed. I was naïve, and hopeful. I didn't think we'd be losing Hammer, the glue that holds us all together. Without him, I don't know who we are, or who I am.

I don't know if I'm a Knight. He's the one who made me feel like I was one of the family. He was the only parent who has ever truly loved me, who wanted the best for me, and now he's gone.

I miss him already.

I also miss myself, because now there's a piece of me gone.

Letting go of Dad's hand, I turn around and cry into Saint's chest.

Hammer's reign as the President of the Knights of Fury MC is over. All the men lower their heads and show their respect.

The Knights' leader is gone.

* * *

I don't leave the clubhouse for two whole weeks. Saint brings me food and tries to force me to eat. I skip my classes, and I don't see my brothers or answer calls from Max, or anyone who I would normally make time for. They try to come to the clubhouse to see me, but I won't see them. Not yet.

I'm a mess.

I've blocked everything and everyone else out, and all I do is keep replaying what happened that day in my head. Could I have done better in the car to help him? I'm training to be a paramedic and I couldn't do anything.

If I'd never fallen for my mother's bullshit, would Hammer still be alive? I cannot believe I went with her. I need help. I must be so desperate for my mother's love that I sacrificed my own father. The whole situation might have played out differently had I not gone with her, and that's what kills me. One little difference could have changed the outcome and Hammer would still be here right now.

The good die young.

Which means my mom is probably going to live forever. If I hated her before, after Hammer's death and the part she played in it, I'll never forgive her as long as I live.

"You need to eat more, Skylar," Saint says, pushing the fruit platter toward me. "I know everyone grieves in their own ways, but you need to take care of yourself. Hammer wouldn't have wanted this."

"Well, he's not here, is he?" I reply, then instantly feel guilty. It's not just me who is grieving—they all loved him and were family to him too. They were here with him all those years I wasn't, and they trusted him above all others.

Saint told me how Hammer pretended he was going to take them all into war but lied to save them, sacrificing himself to get me out of there. He knew what he was going into, but he did it anyway.

The man was fearless.

He didn't want me or any of his men to get hurt, but if he had let them help, he might still be alive. But then again, we might have lost someone else, and I know that wasn't a risk he was willing to take. Like the captain of a ship, he took it as his responsibility and no other's.

And he was the only one left on that sinking ship.

"I'm sorry, Saint. I'm just not myself right now. I'm a mess," I admit, rubbing my eyes. "I just keep thinking about how it didn't need to go this way and driving myself crazy with the what-ifs. And with everything that Mom told me, that's messing my head up too."

I'd told Saint all about everything my mother had shared with me, but I'm not going to tell anyone else. It doesn't matter, and it doesn't change anything.

"I know," he replies, bracing his elbows on his knees and glancing down at the floor. "I keep wishing that I followed him when he said he was going to sort it out. I would have seen him leaving in the car and could have followed him. So I know exactly what you mean, Skylar, but it's not helping. He's gone, and now we have to live with that. We will never forget him. He wasn't just the president of the Knights, he was the founder. He made this family himself."

I open my arms and Saint falls into them. I stroke his back, offering him the comfort he's been giving me this entire time. "You're right, Saint. It's just so hard here without him. I keep expecting him to stick his head inside my room and ask me if I'm hungry, or if I want to come sit outside with him and have a chat."

I know things will get better. When I lost Shauna, I felt exactly like this, and while the pain never goes away, you learn to live with it. You adapt. You survive. You bury that agony, pushing it all the way down until it can resurface only in moments of weakness.

I survived losing my best friend, and I will also survive losing my dad.

It's just going to take me some time before I'm ready to face the world again.

A week later I'm back in classes, playing catch-up because I missed so much that I had to beg not to be kicked out. Using it as the perfect distraction, I bury myself into school and work, keeping myself so busy that I don't have time to think about anything except the task at hand. I finally quit the bar job Hammer always hated, wanting to honor one of the many things he wished for me.

I visit with Logan, Sabrina and all my brothers, who have come to spend time with me. That includes Axel and Smith, who are finally back in town. I fill them all in on what Mom did. I've never seen grown men so upset and sickened before. Logan had to excuse himself and Brooks broke a glass. They couldn't believe everything she had done. Logan tries to remember my biological father, but according to him, my mother had a lot of male "friends" back then.

I love my family, but I don't think I'm going to live with Logan and Sabrina anymore, preferring to be at the clubhouse with Saint now. We talked about getting our own place, but for now, I want to stay. I feel closer to Hammer there, and I love being with Saint every night, and waking up to him every morning.

Life is short, and from now on I'm going to live my life how I want to, not how I'm told I should.

Renny told me that Killer and his two henchmen were on the news, reported as missing people. The abandoned house also somehow caught on fire, and because it's in the middle of nowhere, it was a long time before anyone called the fire department to contain it.

I don't know who actually shot who, and I want to leave it that way. Temper said that if the police come knocking, he already has a plan on how to handle it. I'm guessing if any of us are going to get pinned for the deaths or the fire, it's going to be Hammer. I doubt he'd mind. The fire would have gotten rid of the bodies but not the teeth, so I don't know what Temper did to cover their tracks, but he told me it's all under control and I have nothing to worry about.

The world is better off without Killer and his thugs anyway. I don't know where my mom disappeared to after I saw her, but she wasn't in the house when Saint and the men got there. Bitch is probably back on the farm feeding the horses and pretending she's the quintessential housewife to an unsuspecting Neville. She got what she wanted—Hammer is gone—but I don't think she realized what she was giving up by her selfish actions. All of my brothers have cut contact with her. They've blocked her numbers and told her, in no uncertain words, that they never want to see or speak to her ever again.

I wish I felt satisfaction at that. But I don't. There is no way for me to take legal action against her without implicating the Knights, so that is also out of the question.

I feel nothing when I think of her, other than disappointment mixed with anger.

"Temper is stepping up as our president," Saint tells me one day when we're sitting outside, staring at the sky and having a drink.

I nod. "I thought that would happen. Does that mean you move up to vice president?"

"Yeah," Saint replies, reaching out and touching my arm. "Means I'll be busier, taking care of things for the club, and have more responsibility. Temper wants to reach out and get more members as well. Hammer preferred us to be a smaller, tightknit chapter, but we want to expand. The more people we have behind us, the less likely someone will want to fuck with us. We want to be a force to be reckoned with. Are you going to be okay with all of this?"

"I'm by your side all the way," I say. "And I trust Temper. He will be a great president."

"Good," he replies, exhaling. "I was worried you'd say you wanted out. And I wouldn't blame you. If you didn't want this, I'd leave it for you. So don't think it's ever me and the club or nothing. You are the most important person in my life, and I'm never going to fuck this up. I'm not losing you."

"Thank you for saying that, but I knew what I was getting into with you when I came back, Saint. I'd never ask you to choose between me and the club. I love the club. This is my family, too, and I'm not going anywhere. After Hammer died I felt as though I didn't know if I belong here without him, but I do. As your woman, and more than that too. I love all the men here," I reply, lift-ing my bottle of beer to my lips, then to the sky.

"I love you, Dad," I whisper, smiling sadly.

I can almost hear his voice replying in my head. *I love you too, Sky.*

Chapter Thirty-Two

When the DNA results come in, I'm not surprised. I knew Tory was Saint's the second I saw the photo of her.

I kiss the top of Saint's head as he sits down on his bed, letter in his hand.

"How do you feel?" I ask, smiling down at him. "Carol can no longer say that Tory is not yours whenever she feels like holding that over your head."

"I'm really fucking relieved," Saint admits, placing the piece of paper next to him on the bed. "I love that little girl and it broke my heart when Carol started saying that she wasn't mine. Now I know for sure, and there's nothing she can say. Hunter, my lawyer, said we should get a child custody agreement in place so we have set times to have Tory. This way Carol can't go back on her word and decide one day that she doesn't want to let me see her."

I'm so glad Saint has gotten help from one of the best family lawyers in the city. "That sounds good," I say to him. "It's good if you can come to an agreement out of court, so she doesn't try to bring the whole MC thing into it."

Saint agrees. "Yeah, but it's not like she's mother of the year, and her criminal record is on par with mine."

"You sure know how to pick them," I grumble, sitting down next to him.

"Hey, I picked you, didn't I?" he replies, pushing me back on the bed and pinning my arms above my head. "When are you going to let that go? I didn't make the best choices while you were gone. I didn't think I deserved any better, if I'm being honest, and now I know I have to pay for those decisions, but we got Tory out of it, so I can't have any regrets. And one day I will have more kids with you, the love of my life, and I can't wait for that day."

"I have let it go, but that doesn't mean I'm not allowed to make a little petty comment every now and again," I joke, laughing out loud when he starts to tickle me.

"Yes, actually that's exactly what it means. If you forgive me for my past, it means you can't throw it in my face anymore, even if it's a joke." He clears his throat, and then adds, "It hurts, because I don't like that I let you down, or that I was that person in the first place, the kind who gravitated toward toxic people. I'm not perfect, and trust me, I know that more than anyone."

"I know, Saint," I reply, sobering. "I'm sorry."

"You know, Hammer said something similar to me when he found out Carol was pregnant," Saint admits, smiling sadly, his eyes distant. "He said it's a woman's mentality that raises those kids, nothing else. Not their looks, not how fun or exciting they may be. And that line stuck with me. Because Carol's mentality isn't what I want for Tory. End of the day, she is her mother, though, and now I need to live with that and be civil for Tory."

I nod. "Yeah, you do. Both of your lives are now entwined forever, whether she's the woman you want to raise your child or not. However, I was raised by Georgia, and I turned out okay, so maybe there's hope for everyone."

Saint lowers his face to mine. "Yeah, but you were also raised by Hammer, and everything he taught you, all that time he spent on you, obviously made an impact, because you are amazing."

"From now on, I'll keep quiet and leave your past in the past," I say, not wanting to fight with him again over this. I shouldn't have brought it up again and it was immature of me to do so, when I told myself I would leave it all where it belongs. "If we don't solve this it's just going to keep coming up again and again. It's something I'm going to have to deal with it because I want to be with you forever, and nothing is going to change that." I pause, and then add, "Except cheating."

"I'd never cheat on you," he declares, blue eyes narrowing. "There's no one else I'll ever want, Skylar. I have no doubt about that."

"Good," I say, lifting my head and pressing my lips against his. "And right back at you."

"You better get to class," he murmurs, kissing down my neck. "Which is a shame, because I really want to show you just how much I love you right now."

Grinning, I push him away and get off the bed. "You're right, I'm going to be late otherwise. I'll see you later tonight."

I give him another quick kiss and then head to my car, only for Temper to stop me before I can get in. "Hey," he says, shifting on his feet. "I just had a visit from Hammer's lawyer."

"Hammer had a lawyer?" I ask, eyebrows raising as I throw my handbag on the car seat and turn back to give

Temper my full attention. "I guess you guys would need one. What did he want?"

Temper holds out a bank card to me, one that already has my name on it. "Hammer had this card made for you, as an additional cardholder on his account. If anything happened to him, he had it in his will that all of his money, property and assets go to you. The lawyer said you can start using this right away, that you just need to use the pin code. Do you know it?"

Six, one, seven, three. The numbers he made me memorize. Hammer left everything he owned to a little girl he raised, one who was not of his blood, but of his heart.

"Yeah, I know it," I reply, looking down at the card. "What am I supposed to do with it?"

The thing is, I don't want any of his things or money, and I'd give them all up to have him walk through those clubhouse doors just one more time.

"Whatever you want," Temper says, shrugging. His big build shields me from the sunlight, and I have to look up to speak with him. "Maybe live a life of luxury."

"I don't want to live a life of anything with money I never earned myself," I tell him, feeling a little overwhelmed suddenly. "I don't know what I'm supposed to do with this information."

"There's no rush for you to decide," Temper reminds me, resting his big hand on my slight shoulder. "Just keep it for a rainy day for now, or make it another's day problem. Either way, you'll want for nothing now, Sky. Hammer has you covered for the rest of your life."

"Thanks, Temper. I better get to class. I'm already late, so you're right, I'll just worry about this later."

I wave and jump in the car, thinking about the money

the whole way to the campus. Hammer was so adamant I remember that code, and I thought it would have been for something more important than money, but maybe he just wanted to make sure I was looked after forever. If he couldn't be here to make sure that I was, he's now given me enough money that he will never have to worry.

He loved me so much he planned for this, maybe even expected that one day it would come, considering his lifestyle and who he was. I'm grateful, but I didn't love him for what he could give me. I love him for how he hugged me, made me feel safe and actually listened to me when I had something to say. I mean actually listened, like he had all the time in the world for me every single time I spoke, and that's so rare nowadays. I love him because he put his phone down when he saw me, because he didn't judge me for choosing Saint, because he knew I was nothing like my mother.

I love him because he loved me, and that was it. It was that simple.

Wiping my tears away, I get out of my car and rush to class.

I'm going to make him proud, and I'm going to think of something to do with the money that involves more than shopping and living in luxury. Maybe donate to charity, such as the hospital I used to volunteer at, and of course pay off the rest of my paramedic program. I'd like to buy something for the MC, and save the rest for a rainy day.

"Hey, Skylar," Reece welcomes me as I drop into the seat next to him. "Is everything okay?"

"Yeah," I say, forcing a smile. "At least, it will be."

Knights don't lie down for long.

Epilogue

Glancing up at Max on stage, I smile before turning back to Saint, who has his hands a little too low for my liking, considering everyone is watching us for our first dance as a married couple.

"Can you keep it PG until we're alone?" I whisper, lip twitching. "Your mother is watching us."

"So?" He shrugs, dipping me backward and smiling when everyone starts clapping.

"I'm so glad we did those dance classes," I say, feeling confident as I move with him. "Or else you probably would have almost dropped me like in the lessons."

He kisses me, smiling against my lips. "I'm used to moving with your body in a different way."

"Well, we *are* good at that," I reply, letting him spin me around before pulling me close against his body again. "I think I could get used to seeing you in a suit."

"Prefer this to my leather?" he asks, arching a brow.

"No." But I've never seen him look as handsome as he does right now. The black suit and white shirt fit him like a second skin, and it shows off his build perfectly.

When I walked down the aisle with Temper—I wanted Temper to walk me down the aisle so I didn't have to choose between my brothers, and because Temper was the closest to Hammer—I couldn't stop staring at Saint. I just feel so lucky that I now get to call this man my husband. "But you do clean up very nicely."

"And you're the most beautiful woman I've ever laid my eyes on," he replies, glancing down at my white lace dress. "You always were, Skylar. I'm the luckiest man alive."

"I was just thinking how lucky I am," I say, and we share a look.

This is where I've always meant to be, this is fate, and this man is my soul mate.

Saint dances with Tory next, and it's the cutest thing ever.

"She's adorable," Logan says, offering me his hand. "Can I have the next dance?"

"You may," I say with a smile, accepting it. He leads me to the dance floor where he shows me his skills, which I find quite charming.

"You look so happy, Sky," Logan says, eyes gentle. "After everything you've been through, you're still one of the best people I know, and I'm so proud to be your big brother. I love you."

"I love you, too, Logan," I say to him, my heart full. Mom wasn't invited to the wedding, obviously, and I feel no guilt about that. I don't even know if she is aware that I was getting married, since no one talks to her anymore. I hope she stays away from me and my family.

My brothers, in order of age, all have a dance with me, followed by my adorable nephew Bronson, Logan's son. After I hand him back, Temper takes a turn, his stiff moves making me giggle. "Hammer would be so proud of you right now, Sky," he says quietly. "He loved you so much, you know that, right?"

"I do," I reply. "Thank you for giving me away today. It means everything to me."

"Always stepping in for Hammer," he jokes, leaning forward to kiss my forehead. "Was happy to do it."

Saint steals me back from Temper, and the two of us dance closely, bodies touching.

I've never been happier.

Three Years Later

I've never been more exhausted.

"Why the hell did I decide this was a good idea?" I ask Saint, breathing heavily. "No, wait, this was your idea! Oh my God, it hurts so much, Saint. No amount of orgasms is worth this…"

He strokes my sweaty forehead. "It's fine, Skylar. Just keep breathing."

If he says that to me again, I'm going to attack him. When I came to the hospital, I was already six centimeters dilated, so I couldn't get an epidural, which was what I was hoping for. Instead, I'm feeling childbirth in its full, raw glory, and it's unlike any pain I've ever experienced before.

"There's no way that getting kicked in the balls hurts like this," I tell him, digging my nails into his palm. "I don't have balls, but I just know it. There's no way. Whoever made that up is a man and a dickhead."

Saint, the bastard, laughs out loud at that.

I'm going to murder him.

When I fell pregnant, I was over the moon. I was

already a qualified paramedic, and I love what I do. I will always be grateful to Hammer for suggesting that I should become one. My eyes lit up when I spoke about it, he said, and he was right. I love going in every day and saving as many people as I can. And now when a member of the Knights gets hurt, I'm the first one they call. With my career sorted, and no financial stress on us because of Hammer's money, the timing was perfect to add to our family, to give Tory a sibling and for me to experience being a mother.

"You're doing so well, babe," Saint assures me, moving to glance down at my vagina, which I imagine looks really fucking interesting right now, especially when I feel the baby crown.

"Fuck," he whispers, unable to look away.

He was never at Tory's birth—he arrived after—so this is the first time he's witnessing a baby push out, and going by his expression, it just might be the last.

"Can you look at my face, please?" I cry, pushing with all of my might, using the pain of each contraction to bring my child into the world.

Suddenly I hear crying, and see a thick head of dark hair in Saint's arms. Overwhelmed with emotion but also relieved because I'm no longer in agony, I close my eyes and take a moment. When I open them again, Saint is in front of me, handing me this beautiful bundle of joy.

"We have a son," he says, eyes filled with sentiment, happiness and pride. "He is perfect, Skylar."

My son stops crying as soon as he's laid on my chest. "He really is perfect."

Tears drip down my cheeks, but this time they are happy ones.

"Xavier," I whisper. Same name as Hammer.

Blue eyes open and look directly at me.

And that's when I learn for myself that love at first sight is a very real thing.

* * * * *

Reviews are an invaluable tool when it comes to spreading the word about great reads.
Please consider leaving an honest review for this or any of Carina Press's other titles that you've read on your favorite retailer or review site.

Stay tuned for the next book in the
Knights of Fury MC series,
Renegade,
coming in Fall 2019!
For more information on books
by Chantal Fernando,
please visit her website at
www.authorchantalfernando.com.

Acknowledgments

A big thank-you to Carina Press for working with me on the Knights of Fury MC series!

Thank you to Kimberly Brower, my amazing agent, for having my back in all things.

To my family, my sister Tenielle, and my three sons, thank you for bringing joy to my life every damn day.

And to my readers, thank you for loving my words. I hope this book is no exception.

About the Author

New York Times, Amazon and *USA Today* Bestselling
Author Chantal Fernando is thirty-two years old and
lives in Western Australia. Lover of all things romance,
Chantal is the author of the bestselling books *Dragon's
Lair*, *Maybe This Time* and many more.

When not reading, writing or daydreaming she can
be found enjoying life with her three sons and family.